My Name Is Bosnia

DEC 2006

My Name Is Bosnia

Madeleine Gagnon

Translated by Phyllis Aronoff & Howard Scott

Talonbooks
Vancouver

Copyright © 2005 VLB éditeur and Madeleine Gagnon
Translation copyright © 2006 Phyllis Aronoff & Howard Scott

Talonbooks
P.O. Box 2076, Vancouver, British Columbia, Canada V6B 3S3
www.talonbooks.com

Typeset in Galliard and printed and bound in Canada.

First Printing: 2006

The publisher gratefully acknowledges the financial support of the Canada Council for the Arts; the Government of Canada through the Book Publishing Industry Development Program; and the Province of British Columbia through the British Columbia Arts Council for our publishing activities.

The translators gratefully acknowledge the assistance of the Banff International Literary Translation Centre at the Banff Centre in Banff, Alberta, and of the Canada Council for the Arts.

No part of this book, covered by the copyright hereon, may be reproduced or used in any form or by any means—graphic, electronic or mechanical—without prior permission of the publisher, except for excerpts in a review. Any request for photocopying of any part of this book shall be directed in writing to Access Copyright (The Canadian Copyright Licensing Agency), 1 Yonge Street, Suite 800, Toronto, Ontario, Canada M5E 1E5; tel.: (416) 868-1620; fax: (416) 868-1621.

Je m'appelle Bosnia was first published in French by VLB éditeur, Montreal, in 2005. Financial support for this translation provided by the Canada Council for the Arts and the Department of Canadian Heritage through the Book Publishing Industry Development Program.

LIBRARY AND ARCHIVES CANADA CATALOGUING IN PUBLICATION

Gagnon, Madeleine, 1938–
[Je m'appelle Bosnia. English]
    My name is Bosnia / Madeleine Gagnon ; translated by Phyllis Aronoff & Howard Scott.

Translation of: Je m'appelle Bosnia.
ISBN 0-88922-542-7

    I. Aronoff, Phyllis, date II. Scott, Howard, 1952–
III. Title. IV. Title: Je m'appelle Bosnia. English.

PS8576.A46J413 2006   C843'.54   C2006-901617-8

ISBN-10: 0-88922-542-7
ISBN-13: 978-0-88922-542-8

For Mirheta and her little girl Esma

CONTENTS

We will approach things from the other side to explore the bright face of night.

LORAND GASPAR

Fleeing does not only mean leaving; it also means arriving somewhere.

BERNARD SCHINK

Part One

BOSNIA-HERZEGOVINA

I

"For a long time, I knew happiness."

From deep in her forest with the Bosnian guerrillas and from deep in her young solitude, Bosnia spoke these words to herself and to the entire universe. Did she shout them or whisper them? It didn't matter. But one thing was certain: for a long time, she had known happiness, and she knew it no longer.

She would leave this country, that was certain. To go where? She did not know. But she knew that life itself had abandoned her long before this war. And that, leaving, she would still have the strength to open the back door of life and walk alone into the darkness. The strength, and the courage. She had not constructed a philosophy of despair like the ones in her books at the University of Sarajevo. She had not spent centuries planning the emergency exits by which she could escape, leaping from the earth onto long, soft staircases that lead to pillowy clouds on which you can finally go back to sleep peacefully, and then wake up again one fine morning with a lover in your arms.

She had already had her share of personal tragedy when one day she was thrown by a sudden realization. But unlike the heavenly light that made Paul the Christian fall off his horse on the road to Damascus, her flash of insight came out of such darkness that only the presence of stars in the opaque night kept her from tumbling through the universe. And yet, she had to imagine those stars. She had to revive them, in a sense, through still-warm memory alone, and thanks to them, one certainty remained intact. Turning her back to her country, walking toward her fate as a wandering refugee, she would sum it up this way: if war has existed since the beginning of time, war and torture, rape and pornography of every kind, it is for the simple reason that some human beings, a lot of them, love to kill.

When we have understood that, once and for all, when we've looked that horror in the face, through and through, in all its dimensions, we reach the other slope of sorrow. Suddenly, we know what happiness was. And if it was—this is the paradox—it still is, in a way, or at least it can come back.

It was with the guerrillas deep in the forest that Bosnia came to understand the love of death. It happened after she had buried her father, who had been killed while fighting bravely. She could have been killed too, or raped and carried off as fodder for pleasure and pain, and put in one of the makeshift brothels of the enemy, but fate decided otherwise.

She was coming back with a wild rabbit hanging from her belt. Her father could make really great roast rabbit, and she was imagining his joy at seeing her arrive, proud of what she'd bagged, and how they would savour it, they were so hungry. She was totally caught up in that pleasure when she heard the shot and, moments later, advancing softly through the bushes, saw his body lying in the leaves, his vacant eyes and the trickle of blood running from his ear down his neck. She saw the prints of their boots and, beside his still-warm hand, the shell from that lethal cartridge, which she flung away with all her strength, but without shrieks or tears; she wanted everything to be softness and silence to accompany the great crossing to the beyond that, without knowing why, she imagined to be serene.

Bending down to close his eyelids, she saw on his cheekbone a little bump of skin she had never noticed, like a teardrop of flesh—on someone who in life had wept so little. For him, she tried to remember the verses of the Koran on death. Few words came up out of the darkness—she hadn't set foot in a mosque since what happened so long ago. Strange, but it was to the sound of a Bach partita rising to her ear from the labyrinth within that this single phrase for her dead father came to her lips: "In the Name of God, the All-Mothering, the Merciful."

She remembered then that in one of her philosophy courses at the University of Sarajevo, perhaps the course on Plato, the professor had explained to them that the pre-Islamic god was a female figure, as shown by the etymology of *Al-Lat*. As she chanted that single sentence that had come back to the sound of a few bars of the Bach partita, her father in death, with his teardrop of flesh, became like a mother, and she could bury him in peace, placing the wild rabbit beside him in the grave she had dug with her bare hands for a feast in the beyond. "You never know," she said to herself, thinking that this contentment that now seemed to be his would perhaps deliver his wife from the madness that had befallen her at the beginning of the war. That woman who had been so alive, so vivacious and loving, was now walled up in the great silence of the psychiatric asylum, and in her own silence. "Mama, come back," she said very softly as she buried her father.

In the forest with the guerrillas, through the love of her father now gone away to an eternity of enigmas, Bosnia understood, once and for all, the love of death that has moved murderers since the beginning of time. And through her father, who with his teardrop of flesh had become an Al-Lat mother, she finally reached the other slope of sorrow, where you can remember happiness and, through memory, make it exist. Where you can leave from and, if you want, go around the world without dying. She had this illumination out of the most opaque darkness, the darkness that alone allows you to see the stars.

Before leaving her country, before becoming a wandering refugee, she would go back to the psychiatric hospital in Sarajevo to give her mother a hug. Despite her certainties, born of the fields of desolation, she still wondered what madness was.

And Bosnia murmured to herself, "My poor mother, although I don't understand her, I'll take her in my arms. I'll sing her a lullaby about how her man Ismet has become a saint for all eternity, a hero. I'll sing to her that Ismet had no woman but her. And he loved no one but us—her, my brother, me. I'll tell her that, one day, when she's cured of the sorrow of living, I'll come back with my brother to take her to a land of peace that I am going away to find."

In the deep forest, she suddenly understood the love of death, death that is given and death that is received.

Unable to prepare her father's body, she buried him anyway with the sacred chant that had come up from the dark labyrinth of her soul, acting as *bula*.* And so she reached a stage in life at which enigmas finally seem to be solved.

Having for months worn her combat outfit of jeans, sweater, parka, and close-cropped hair, a dagger in her belt (her father had given it to her when they had decided to join the guerrillas), Bosnia couldn't wear the veil either, as required for a normal funeral ceremony, but with this war, nothing was normal any more. Out of respect, she made the gesture of covering her head with an invisible piece of sheer fabric in her trembling hands. Though for a very long time she had not believed in God or the Devil or put on that symbol of the religion for which they were being massacred in their peaceful houses and gardens, she promised her father from this imaginary position that she would wear the scarf when she went back down into their vale of sorrow.

---

* Muslim woman who embalms the body.

She made this promise as if, with her father's death, she was espousing the beliefs of the fathers and grandfathers he'd told her so much about. About the mothers and grandmothers, he'd told her nothing. It was her mother who had talked to her about them— that was the tradition.

Now, at this stage of solved enigmas, that at least was how, in a flash of understanding, she saw the human love of death: with the remembered verse of the female Al-Lat and the music of Bach resonating in the inner labyrinth as she made that promise to her buried father. Without tears. Ready for the struggle of life that awaited her.

She decided to leave her country. To go where there was no war. The world was full of countries at peace, despite appearances. She wondered what the struggle of life consisted of there, where it did not lead inevitably to killing. Was it even possible?

II

SHE HAD ADOPTED THE NAME Bosnia when she decided to leave Bosnia-Herzegovina. Not that she hated her old name, Sabaheta, but she did find it a bit old-fashioned, and in leaving, she felt this desire to become a new person. By calling herself Bosnia, she was giving herself a new life without betraying the old one, she was leaving her country without abandoning it completely.

Leaving is dying a little, dying to oneself. And it is living fully as that other person one has so often dreamed of becoming. While one has to leave for elsewhere in order to achieve this, it is at home that the dream is first imagined. For Sabaheta, to call herself Bosnia elsewhere would be to pay tribute to here, where the dream had taken root.

While she knew what her new name was to be, she did not yet have a clear idea of where she would go. While waiting, she would go down to Sarajevo, and every day, if possible, she would go to the psychiatric hospital and take her mother in her arms, speak to the mute she had become, cradle her, sing her songs, wash her, and comb her long dull grey hair. She would wait for the end of the war, or the end of time if there was no time other than the time of war. She would wait, and then she would comfort her mother for the death of her Ismet and the death of everything.

Without her father at her side, she would no longer fight, that was decided. To fight, she would have had to go with the men in the guerrillas, but without her father, she no longer had any protection—to her former comrades, her woman's body would become a territory to be ravaged, a shelter to be broken into, a house to be pillaged, a meal to be devoured. It had always been this way. She had known rape as soon as her child's body had become a woman's. She hadn't even had time to anticipate her adult life when it was nipped in the bud. It was in her own body, still that of a child, that she had first learned of war.

She would wait for the end of the war, or the end of time, and then she would leave. To go where? She did not know exactly. But she understood that once there, another self within her might live, one she now dreamed of under the name Bosnia.

She would wait for her mother to get better—who knows, madness is such a mystery. Wherever she found herself after the war, she would study psychology—and maybe medicine—in order to better understand the diseases of the mind. And if her mother got better, she would take her to that country of new beginnings, that was certain. Otherwise, she would have to leave her behind, because she couldn't imagine any country opening its doors to the madness of others—other countries had enough madness of their own.

Since she no longer had a place to live, she would go and see if her friends from the University of Sarajevo were still alive. She would go knock on the doors of Adila, Esma, and Amila, and ask them at least for a place to sleep and something to wash with and a little something to eat, she was so hungry. She would start with Adila, because, before the war, they had lived together during the school year in a tiny but pretty apartment. Other than that, she had always lived with her parents in a house in a village at the edge of the forest, not very far from Tuzla. At the beginning of the war, the house had been razed and the crops burned. At first, they'd hidden with neighbours and friends, who happened to be on the right side—they were from the same ethnic group and the same religion as the conquering enemies, the two went together—and then one day, or rather one night, they'd had to flee. Their presence there had become too dangerous for everyone.

They had travelled over hills and through valleys, enduring innumerable ordeals, and had finally managed to reach Sarajevo, where their people were in the majority, and where they had naively believed that after being driven from their homes, they would now be left in peace. It seemed she no longer wanted to remember how they did it, there were so many snares, so many sorrows. Bosnia told herself that one day, in the country of calm new beginnings, when she had slowly recovered from everything she'd been through, she would review the events of those campaigns of hostilities, one by one, she would consider them and analyze them, the better to assimilate them. She remembered a class on catharsis in Greek tragedy, which her professor, the distinguished Lutvo H., had related to a concept of Freud's. But she had forgotten her professor's argument. Like the professor himself, who had been killed by a sniper at the beginning of the siege of Sarajevo, the argument had vanished.

No, Bosnia did not want to remember now. Totally taken up with survival, she felt that before leaving, for the sake of her health and maybe even the restoration of her mother's health, it was her duty to forget.

Also, despite all logic, she was still waiting for her brother, Mumo, her elder by four years. He'd been her best friend before the war, her most loyal ally, she'd called him "Mumo, my twin." Against all logic, because he had been kidnapped at the very beginning of the hostilities. He was coming back from the river with his catch of trout when he had surprised the paramilitaries looting the house and buildings before burning them and killing anything that moved—cows, rabbits, dogs, and cats, even birds. Some neighbours had seen them hurl themselves upon Mumo, beat him, tie him up, and throw him into their tarp-covered truck with the tools. A neighbour recounted how at first Mumo had tried to hide the fish, which were hanging from a branch, in his knapsack, as if he hadn't yet realized what was happening, as if keeping them from getting his fish could magically hold back the war. Another neighbour told of seeing Mumo's incredulous look from his hiding place: "Your brother at that moment looked like the little boy who used to come and play at our house when he was six years old." And he added, "You know very well, little Sabaheta, that they slaughtered him. Come now, robust, vigorous young men like him make the best targets for a Kalash." But Sabaheta did not want to admit it.

So Bosnia was still waiting for Mumo's return.

"I'm waiting for Mumo's return," she reflected. "I'm waiting for the end of the war. I'm waiting for the end of my mother's madness. Through the brambles, the underbrush, the forest, the streams, the rocks to climb, the hiding places, through the dangers, the fear and the cold, the hunger, and the terror, I'm waiting to reach the top of one of the seven hills, from which I will see Sarajevo, the city that I love, that one day I will leave, I'm waiting to go down into it one dark night, to slip into its entrails sticky with blood, into its belly burning with fire, I'm waiting as I walk."

One night, trying to fall asleep in the foxhole she had dug, with two sheets, a pillow, and a duvet made of the stuff of the earth and its leafy trees, she reflected that her bed was truly luxurious. Because of the cold, she had only left an opening for her eyes, nose, and mouth, which had required an infinite amount of meticulous work. From where she was lying, she saw the moon all full and blue through the branches creaking in the wind, and she was filled with gratitude for this bed, this earth, this moon and sky. She thought of her brother Mumo, who would be brought back by a miracle, and of her father, resting forever in the same ground, and she suddenly remembered Giono, whose books she had loved to read in her French literature classes in high school, and whose words, from *Harvest* or *Hill of*

Destiny, she had learned by heart and recited, and she thought, "Provence, that's where I'd like to go."

Then, before going to sleep, she began to name those countries in the books that had opened the doors to her dream of leaving. France, because French had been her first choice of a language to learn, because it was foreign yet not too distant. France, for the love she had felt for its literature since the beginning. England, because English had given her Shakespeare, Joyce, Dylan Thomas, and the Rolling Stones (she remembered with delight the year she'd spent in Great Britain in a posh college on a government scholarship when Yugoslavia was still united). Egypt, because of the pyramids, the Nile, and Durrell's *Alexandria Quartet*, and because she wanted to know at least one Arab country and to meet her co-religionists, they would surely be more sympathetic to her cause—this she dreamed, but did she in fact have a cause? Then she thought of the Canadian North, the land of ice and of the Inuit and Innu, where there had never been a war, never been blood on the white breast of the land—except that of the caribou and the seals that they killed while praying, just to survive, and that of the women giving birth in igloos. She had only read stories of the Canadian North, its vast spaces and the freedom of its time slowly counted out in winter.

She was waiting, and that night before sinking into sleep, she wondered if the waiting was part of the journey. Waiting, wasn't that already leaving?

III

The morning Bosnia reached Sarajevo, it was very calm. Had the enemy in the hills decamped or were they all dozing? Could the war be over? But isn't the end of a war something that is proclaimed? With these questions and more in her mind, she made her way, exhausted, through the streets and alleys of her sleeping city.

Dawn brought her a threefold happiness. First of all, she was back in her city, the city she had fled with her father in terror of shells, fire, and snipers, after taking her mother, who had been screaming and delirious for weeks, to the psychiatric hospital. Second, seeing the green thread of light on the horizon, she realized she would witness the birth of another day, and the birth of the day is the beginning of life, that's what she felt every time the light reappeared. And finally, her pockets were stuffed with hazelnuts, which she had been munching on and savouring like a happy squirrel since she had passed through a stand of hazelnut trees yesterday at dusk.

She looked at the sky soft as cotton fleece, enjoying the crunch of the hazelnuts in her mouth. Although she didn't know how to pray and had never gone to a *mualimah,** she began to chant her Al-Lat to the vastness: "In the Name of God, the All-Mothering, the Merciful." She had cramps in her belly because of her period. She vaguely remembered an erotic dream she'd had the night before, lying in the warm hazelnut grove in the moist odour of the fall humus, she had forgotten the details of the dream and even the characters who visited her, all she had was an inner image of softness and kindness. She looked at the dawn sky, like the belly of a woman whose waters of snow were about to break—every year since she was very little, she could sense the first snow before it came, it was a gift. Content, she continued walking, her gait lithe, silent. She remembered reading in her children's books that this was how the Amerindians walked in the forest, stealthily, without the slightest crack of a twig, so as not to be detected. She felt light. Her city lay at her feet. As if in moss slippers, she slipped into it in a state of weightlessness.

She had never believed in eternity, but in that early morning, heaven for her was a hazelnut to be savoured, and the sky, a womb that would open, spilling rivers of milk in the form of starry flakes.

She walked amid the sounds of the awakening city: the snorting of motors turning over, the creaking of

---

* Muslim woman responsible for religion lessons.

cartwheels and wobbly bicycles, the snap of wood breaking in the hands of people scavenging for fuel, muffled yapping and meowing—the animals were intelligent and had learned since the shortages to make themselves scarce to potential hunters lurking everywhere—the whoosh of the wings of the remaining pigeons and doves. But there were no calls to prayer from up in the minarets or bells tolling in the cathedrals and churches, and the humans she glimpsed scurried like shadows to those little tasks that would ensure their survival for at least another day (she recalled a phrase from Saint-Exupéry: "What was a man's life worth … ? Ten seconds, perhaps; or twenty"). From the total absence of human voices, Bosnia knew that Sarajevo was still at war. It was worrying, this silence. It was heavy. Just as alarming as the noise and tumult she had left in terror, with her father. Could this aphasia of the city have given speech back to her mother, who had become mute under the tumult and cacophony of the weapons?

Bosnia continued on towards Adila's apartment, which wasn't much farther. She hoped, oh how fervently she hoped, that she would find the building intact and her faithful friend alive! Through the streets and alleys, every turn seemed like a trap, as if everything foreboded her death. Suddenly, she heard something rolling at her feet. She held her breath and saw an apple rolling downhill over the cobblestones. An apple, a real apple! She hadn't eaten an apple in three moons— that's how she counted the months, lacking a calendar. She wanted so much to avoid notice, she moved along the sidewalk to the fruit like a puppet suspended from invisible strings. Thinking of the Bible story of the forbidden fruit, she snatched it up and hid behind a shed to savour every last fibre of it down to the flesh of the seeds, which she found incredibly delicious. She said to herself that maybe it didn't take a war for miracles, but, "name of no-God"—as Giono, her favourite writer, would say—that was good. Stendhal, Kafka, and Dostoyevsky were also favourites, but she had never been able to learn a single sentence of theirs by heart.

Walking towards the centre of Sarajevo on the other side of the Miljacka River, which she would have to be very careful crossing, she thought about the books she had missed so much since her flight into the forest, whose words had come back to her in the loneliness and danger of the nights and helped her to live, words she had recited like incantations to ward off the evil spell of death all around. She was eager to find them, not knowing yet that they would help her keep from freezing to death that winter when she and her companions in misfortune, lacking wood, would have to burn them one by one to keep warm, not knowing yet that having to choose which book to burn first would be an appalling mental torture and that, to keep from going mad, they would each learn chapters by heart and recite them by the fire.

And then, as in a film that has suddenly been slowed down or a dream in which a single scene sheds light on the whole story, she found herself in front of the door of her building. There it was. Nothing had changed, there weren't even any tiles broken, the façade and the windows were the same, only the entrance was strewn with debris—old motors, chunks of wood, garbage and refuse everywhere—but the building, in the midst of the forest of ruins, was still intact. "Another miracle," thought Bosnia, tiptoeing through the vestibule, which had become a huge, dank garbage can—drops of liquid trickled down the walls and a starving cat she didn't recognize leapt from a crate and bounded terrified down the dark corridor towards the basement with its rats. Bosnia stood frozen, transfixed. Her whole body began to tremble, and it occurred to her that the forest with its wolves baying at the moon, its lost bears, and its maddened hunters on the lookout for any enemy human beast might be more hospitable than these dwellings that had been built by human hand to be safe shelters but had in wartime become evil lairs where prey is run to ground between life and death. Shivering, she said to herself, "This must be what hell is, these once-welcoming places that have been transformed, as in a nightmare, into places of horror, these buildings created to provide protection and warmth that the reign of war has turned into ghastly hiding places where all you can do is wait in fear and trembling for life to end. Yes, hell is war."

And she could no longer stand waiting for this bad dream to end. She wanted to scream, to howl like an animal, to throw herself into the basement through the forbidding trapdoor, to go and die there among the starving cats and dogs and the rats. But she did not scream. In Bosnia's heart, there still remained a little light that told her to survive, and she once again heard those words of Saint-Exupéry (what book had she read them in? She would see when she found their student bookshelves again, in Adila's apartment, she hoped more than ever that Adila was there alive): "What was a man's life worth … ? Ten seconds, perhaps; or twenty." Her teeth chattering, Bosnia whispered those words, which she found both consoling and depressing. Consoling, because in spite of everything, they held beauty and hope. Depressing, because they envisioned only twenty seconds of life, while she, Sabaheta-Bosnia, imagined an eternity of life for herself. Despite the horror of the tragedy all round, there were mountains of discoveries and joys that, even now, she imagined for herself and for everyone she loved or would love.

Standing in the darkest corner of the icy vestibule, she vowed that she would work all her life, after the war and after her studies, as far away as possible from the battlefields—she did not yet know where or how—somewhere where there were fields of reconciliation as far as the eye could see. For the first time since the death of her brother Mumo and the madness of her mother Anna and the death of her father Ismet, she felt droplets flowing down her cheeks like those on the cracked walls, and they warmed her. Incredulous, she wondered, "Are these tears?"

IV

BOSNIA TOUCHED, then tasted the warm rivulets on her cheeks. Yes, they were tears, those tiny salty streams that do not come down from the mountaintops but rather rise up from the depths of the earth—where, when she was little, she was taught hell was, with its devils and fires—from her own depths, from her burning belly that flowed downward in red waters and upward in white salty waters—she had always known, and she knew it even more clearly today, that there was a true paradise there, her own heaven, private and sovereign, which she touched to warm her hands and calm the cramps from hunger and her period. Despite this gesture to comfort herself, Bosnia knew that the paradise of her belly also contained sorrows and pains, and, taking the immeasurable measure of this paradoxical state of an earthly heaven made of joys shot through with misfortune and woe, a heaven of her own, fragile and powerful, she let the sobs come—a torrent she had been holding back since the shell had fallen on the Markale market in the old Muslim city, killing a hundred and forty civilian victims, including her beloved Aunt Elmedina.

After this overflow of waters carrying the debris of memories and tattered anecdotes, she felt ready to climb the five flights of stairs. To give herself courage, she would count the steps, exactly eighty-five, as she remembered. She wiped her nose with the big leaves of chestnut trees with which she always filled her pockets, once again caressed her warm belly, and made another vow: "One day, after the war and after my studies, somewhere else, very far away from here, with a boy I will love and cherish, with a man who personifies goodness, I will have a child." That thought calmed her.

Starting up the stairs, she remembered another sentence from Giono: "The world is wide for those who, in addition to the earth, still have all the clouds to scale." She no longer knew which character had said these words, but this gap in her memory mattered little. What counted was the truth of the words.

On the first landing, she thought again of love. It had been so long since she had met any young men that weren't armed.

On the second, she reflected that between the rape when she was fourteen and now, her youth had passed by like a shadow.

On the third, she sat down, out of breath. There was a great emptiness in her head.

On the fourth, she stumbled, braced herself against the banister, and saw a woman she did not know coming down.

And at the very top, she didn't remember knocking on the familiar door, but she would never forget the ravaged, frightened face of her friend Adila, into whose arms she collapsed.

She woke up on a little metal cot, felt the mattress under her body, ran her hands over clean clothes she didn't recognize—"Such comfort!" she had time to say out loud before sinking back into sleep. In a dream, she felt an inconsolable sorrow: she wanted to bring Adila a little bouquet of flowers as she used to, but she crisscrossed the entire country from north to south and east to west and there were no more flowers anywhere. Exhausted by the futile quest, she awoke again with the words "War kills human beings, animals, and birds. But also all the flowers and bees." "All the flowers," she repeated, barely able to articulate, although in her head it was clear. "War kills all the flowers and bees."

Then some sentences from Ivo Andrić* came back to her from her childhood memories of when their father would recite long passages from Andrić's *Bosnian Chronicle* to her and Mumo and she would fall asleep thinking of Belgrade, which she imagined to be the most beautiful of cities at the end of a fabulous journey. "Will you take us there one day?" they would ask their father. "Of course," he would promise. "With your mother and maybe your Aunt Elmedina. I'll buy a new car, and we'll eat in little inns, there are lots of them

—

* Bosnian writer, winner of the Nobel Prize for literature in 1961.

along the route. I have a friend there who will put us up in his boarding house. Ah Belgrade! Beograd, the White City," he would add as if under a spell. "The Sava River and the Danube, where I'll take you on a boat ride. I know captains whose grandfathers fought side-by-side with mine. Together, they defeated the Ottoman armies and drove them from the country for good." Thinking of what Belgrade had become for her family, and of the fact that in her veins, too, there flowed Turkish blood and that her Muslim religion forbade her from disavowing the former Ottoman conquerors, she was suddenly gripped with terror at the complexity of humanity and woke up fully.

Adila was busy in the kitchen area. And an angel with sunshine hair and water-green eyes was gazing at Bosnia with gentle earnestness. "My name is Marina, I am your friend Adila's second cousin. The war brought me here. I'll tell you about it." She gave Bosnia a little water and asked if she was hungry. Then came Adila's voice: "You'll see, my little Sabaheta. We'll take good care of you. We'll put some flesh back on your bones." Bosnia clearly recognized her motherly friend. It was not surprising that she was studying to be a midwife. Bosnia felt reassured, and at the same time, she thought of her own mother, and wept again. Since those floodgates had reopened, there was a continuous torrent that could no longer be stemmed, as if she was going to cry till the end of her days and die at the end of her sorrow. Was Adila reading her thoughts? She said, "Don't worry about your mother. I go to see her as often as possible. As soon

as the roads are open, when there's no shelling, no fires
crackling in the neighbourhood, no bullets whistling
over our heads, I go. She's still not talking, but she
seems calm, freed of her fears, she doesn't seem to be
suffering any more. Stop worrying, my little ghost from
the forest. When you're better, we'll go together to see
your mama." And the ghost explained to them why,
from now on, her name was Bosnia.

To remind them that horror still reigned in Sarajevo,
there was a roar of shells in the distance. Windowpanes
shattered in the building across the street. Then there
were dull noises, crackling sounds like giant matches,
screams, a woman yelling, the death rattle of a
slaughtered animal, followed by a silence so heavy that
it felt like night in the middle of the day, everlasting
night in this first morning of the winter, which promised
to be eternal. Suddenly the first snowflakes appeared
in the window. There was no wind, and the snow was
falling straight down, very fine. "I would like to be that
peaceful sky," Bosnia thought, "and no longer this
rumbling belly at the centre of the enraged earth."

Then she saw a large basin of pink water on the floor,
and realized that her friends had washed her from head
to foot. She remembered all the blood she had lost. She
had no more cramps in her belly and she felt herself
floating in the soft bed. The black horror of the shelling
outside, the whiteness of the eternal snow falling
silently in white lines, and the water pink with her own
blood came together in her mind, and she thought that
maybe in that place where she was going, which she

imagined as peaceful and distant, she would be a painter after all. To remember precisely this dawn of furies and gentleness she had just experienced.

She was hungry.

And as it happened, the soup was ready.

In time of war, you eat what you can, and what you find. But still, there were big red beans, cabbage, and potatoes. Into this soup, they dunked a kind of dry biscuit made only of flour and water, but still, it was better than nothing. Marina, the blonde angel, began to talk about herself. She said she was the daughter of a Catholic Croat father who hadn't been seen since well before the war; one day, he had gone back to Croatia with a new wife the same age as Marina, abandoning her mother, who was a fundamentalist Muslim, and whose family had forced Marina to marry a businessman from Beirut. The businessman had come to Bosnia-Herzegovina only once, to marry Marina, and had immediately left with her for Saudi Arabia, where he had a "diamond business," he said. She never saw any diamonds, but she discovered that his millions came from trafficking in arms, heroin from Afghanistan, and human flesh (he ran one of the biggest prostitution rings in Western Europe). In the beginning, he loved her, but he soon lost interest, especially since she didn't give him any children. He went out every evening, and had what he referred to as his "sexual adventures" elsewhere, and when he came home, usually drunk, he would beat her, call her a slut, and shout that he wanted a son from her: "A male heir, do you hear me, you empty vessel, dry ground, whore of the desert with a nice ass? You look like a saint, but Allah is punishing you for all your hidden sins." And he would hit her. She dreamed of killing him, but she had no idea how to kill someone.

Bosnia told of her weeks in the forest with her father. Then her father's death. Then the terrors and pleasures of the forest.

There was no wood left for the fire. Telling their stories kept them warm. Soon, Adila and Marina would go out to look for fuel and food. They spent most of each day on these hazardous expeditions. Bosnia still needed to rest. She would try to sleep. At least, when you sleep, you no longer feel hunger, she thought as she listened to her friends' footsteps going down the stairs. Her last thought before falling asleep again was this: "What could I find elsewhere that I don't have here?"

V

BOSNIA WAS AWAKENED by footsteps and laughter on the stairs. She recognized her two friends. It seemed to her that laughter came from another world, and that these joyous outbursts belonged to a strange theatre that she had not attended in ages. Adila and Marina came in with a happy commotion, as if they were little girls again, one carrying a shopping basket loaded with food, and the other dragging a big bundle of wood at the end of a rope. Out of breath and still filled with wonder, they unloaded their treasures in front of the incredulous eyes of Bosnia, who barely remembered that only yesterday, before the war, such riches were commonplace.

There were apples, olives, coffee, almonds, tomatoes, oil, onions, pasta, rice, potatoes, even a chicken, and even a bottle of raki concealed in old newspapers. Marina also produced two packs of cigarettes from the pocket of her jacket. It would be a feast, a celebration, a real party. Bosnia, a bit shaky, got up from her little metal cot, and they started dancing and singing a tune from their childhood, whose words were partly forgotten but went something like this: "Thank you, life / Don't go away, we're coming / Thank you, heaven / Don't disappear, we love you."

And where had all these good things come from?

Three times during their expedition, Adila and Marina had had to take refuge in basements because of heavy shelling. As usual, they had seen frightened creatures scurrying with them into the shelters, each one stranger than the next: a distraught mother with a rickety baby hanging from her empty breast, a dishevelled grandmother screaming insults in all directions, a brute of a husband dragging his wife by her shawl and continuing the volley of blows he had begun at home (and what was this able-bodied man doing here, who was supposed to be at war or in prison or dead?), and two young girls holding each other by the hand, weeping softly for this insane humanity in which their lives were beginning.

The miracle occurred in the third shelter. Its name was Adem and its face was that of Bosnia's, Esma's, and Adila's best friend at university. What was he doing in that Sarajevo cellar? Where had he come from? Still trembling (with fear? with cold?), he took Adila's hand in his own cracked hand and held it during the long hour they had to wait, and told her very softly—you must never tell secrets to anyone in these crowded and anonymous places—to follow him to the exit of the building and he would tell her something. She introduced Marina to him, barely whispering "she's my friend." There's no need to show pedigrees in the solidarity among victims of war. In that pause in time—

that's how they experienced their wait in the shelter—
when few people spoke, and they could hear droplets
falling from the wet ceiling, and they were almost afraid
that huge unseen stalactites would fall on their heads in
the darkness, Adila thought of those cracks in Adem's
hands. And she imagined with horror the sessions of
torture that had left his skin all scarred and lacerated.
She learned outside that there was nothing crazy about
what she had imagined. It was true. The Chetniks had
done to Adem what they usually did to Muslims. In her
mind, Adila the midwife suddenly saw the Muslim
bodies of the Bosnian war as so many torn manuscripts,
so many documents archived for the future trials of
criminals. But would they ever take place, those trials?
Would they all live that long? Would there be justice on
this earth or would they have to wait for the Last
Judgment promised in eternity?

(How strange life is! The next morning, shelling
destroyed the Sarajevo National Library and real
Bosnian manuscripts and books went up in smoke. You
couldn't imagine a more terrible ordeal by fire. Adila
was amazed at the coincidence. Only yesterday, she'd
imagined the bodies of her people filing by in the
millions in the form of archival documents, under the
angry gaze of the Eternal at the Last Judgment.)

Adem had promised to come over later to celebrate
with the three of them—if he didn't run into any
obstacles, of course. It was he who, through a contact
he could not reveal, had found the food in an empty
apartment. He'd gone there with Adila and Marina
when they had left the dark shelter. He walked them

back to their building, telling them nervously that he had a lot of things to do. And they watched him run alongside the façades of the gutted buildings, his head hunched down and his feet nimble, until he disappeared into a dark alley, a fleeting shadow for whom this city seemed no longer to hold any secrets.

(Later, after the war, to pay for his studies in law, Adem would organize tours of the Sarajevo ruins for tourists from all over the world, who would marvel at these postmodern sculptures that caught the play of light and shadow in the slanting rays of the sun. In his profound loneliness amid the human vanity and the flashes of the cameras, Adem would hear an untranslatable lyric poem coming from these architectural skeletons, each one recounting a tragic event, transporting him back to the human figures forever departed.)

The three girls had a smoke. How good it was, that Marlboro—where had Adem's contact managed to unearth such manna? Let's not ask any questions, they thought, let's just smoke! Eyes closed in deep meditation, they savoured the effects of the sweet smoke in perfect silence. They had not smoked much before the war, but the lack of it created an insidious need—a well-known fact. After that sublime moment of communion, they got to work on the tasks for the day's celebration, Marina at the hearth and Adila at the stove. She would roast the chicken with onions and potatoes, since salt and pepper and all spices had long since disappeared from the country. As an appetizer, they would have tomatoes in oil with olives, and they'd nibble on almonds with their aperitif of raki. "Careful," said Adila the midwife, "we have to keep some of everything for tomorrow and the following days." That was understood. The other two were familiar with the demands of rationing, but so as not to offend the devoted Adila, who could sometimes be a bit bossy, they kept quiet, smiling knowingly at each other.

Bosnia went back to her bed, not yet strong enough to help with the chores. After all, she had only emerged from her forest early that morning, although, with all the sleeping she'd done, the time seemed to pass more slowly here than outside. She picked up the old newspaper the bottle of raki had been wrapped in and realized it was in fact only three days old. It was from Slovenia and written in Serbo-Croatian—their language—and it recounted in great detail their war in Bosnia-Herzegovina. From elsewhere, but not actually very far away, they would finally learn what was happening here. Bosnia started to read out loud. The three of them were stunned. "Good God, there's suffering and burning throughout the country as far as Croatia," said Marina, shocked. Her only family left now was that of her Croat father and the half-sisters and half-brother she did not know. During all her years away in Saudi Arabia and Lebanon, she had imagined them happy, as well as beautiful, warm, and charming, and loving toward her when she would see them again. But now, she saw them all living through the same sorrows, the same miseries as she was, if they were not already dead under torture—something Adem's mutilated body had reminded her of. Once the fire was going, she sat down on the edge of Bosnia's bed, and Bosnia continued reading.

She went on until Marina collapsed in tears. It was too much for her, the drop of water that burst the dam. Adila rushed over to the bed. The three of them hugged and wept hot tears together. They rocked each other, no longer speaking. The war became a litany of sorrows on Bosnia's iron cot. Then, through the curtain of tears, Adila said to Bosnia, "You know, Marina and I love each other." And they burst into laughter. "Lucky to love," thought Bosnia.

"How about opening the bottle of raki while we wait for Adem?"

VI

"I NEVER WANT TO FORGET this November evening," Bosnia said to herself, watching her two friends eating and drinking raki and laughing and dancing to the tunes of imaginary waltzes while she stoked the fire and relived in her mind the celebrations they used to have in her village before the catastrophe. "I never want to forget these precise moments in November, I want to etch them in my mind forever. I no longer want to remember the horror that has taken over all our lives, I no longer want to think about the rapes, about the dead we did not have time to mourn. I need life, quiet, love, and beauty." Her head was spinning slightly from the raki. It was good. She wanted more. The three of them refilled their empty glasses. Intoxication transported them elsewhere, far from bombs and bullets. The night was bright with stars, and there was no more screaming outside. Perhaps the war had ended unannounced, just as it had begun—no one had seen it coming, they did not know where or how it had all begun.

Bosnia, Adila, and Marina had begun the festivities at nightfall. Adem did not come, but they did not want to worry. Since the beginning of the conflict, there was enough suffering to endure when tragedy struck, and they had learned not to dwell on the unknown. Their survival instinct had taught them the simple wisdom of reserving pain for known misfortune. Adem might come this evening, or tonight or another day. In these tumultuous times, it was never possible to make precise appointments. Events determined your schedule, not the clock. Adem might come and he might not. If he came, he had promised to bring another bottle of alcohol, and the party would go on. If he didn't come, or if he never came, there would be plenty of days of darkness and rage to mourn one more death.

"I don't want to think that Mumo is dead, I don't want to believe he's gone forever. When I'm better, I'll go see Mama and I'll begin investigations to track Mumo down. I'll become a detective, I'll become the Simenon of Bosnia-Herzegovina—there's a reason I love his books. No Serb will be able to avoid my search. I'll disguise myself as a cleaning woman or I'll dye my hair blonde and curl it like the loose women of Belgrade—no, I'll look innocuous and anonymous. I'll cover the whole country, I'll gather clues, I'll overcome every obstacle, I'll leave no stone unturned, and I'll succeed, I'll find my brother, my twin, my Mumo, even if I have to become a prison guard for the Serbs and dress as a boy the way I did in the guerrillas with my father." Bosnia touched the tip of the dagger she always carried in her belt, even in bed. Sliding her fingers over the smooth, sharp blade, she wondered why it was so difficult for girls to kill. Why it had always been so. And why they were still being raped. She imagined herself leading commandos of women patrolling all over the world, emasculating the rapists of women and children.

The laughter of her friends drew her from her reverie. The two lovers came over and sat on Bosnia's cot and snuggled together under the good old wool blanket. Bosnia put another log in the fireplace and joined them. They took little gulps of the last of the raki. The great silence outside blanketed the secrets of the universe, leaving the indoors to its own music, the *dolce pianissimo* crackling of the fire.

Marina began to tell her story. She spoke at length about her tribulations as a young bride—she was eighteen years older than Bosnia and Adila, having been born in 1954, and had been eighteen years old when the marriage was negotiated between the two families and Asim came to take her to Saudi Arabia. In that July of 1972, they could not have begun to imagine the war and the dismantling of Yugoslavia. She told of her first night with Asim, when, trembling with fear, she had to open her legs and let him ram his sex into her like a weapon, and she lost consciousness under the assault. Her mother had told her she would suffer, but she could not have imagined how much. During that animal onslaught, while he went at her, screaming that she was his whore, his thing, his slave, Marina for the first time in her life had an insane desire to bite, to tear out the hair of this brute to whom she had vowed

46

obedience and faithfulness in front of the imam; for the first time, she lost her faith in the Eternal. For the first time, too, she wanted to kill. It was in this chasm of hatred that she became a woman.

She bled for days and did not want Asim to touch her ever again. When he approached, she would howl like a beast. The more he forced her, the meaner she felt herself becoming. She understood the lionesses and she-wolves and all the wild she-beasts of the world. She stopped taking care of her beauty—oh yes, she knew she was beautiful, she had been told so often since she was very small, and even Asim had been in thrall to her charms, as he whispered to her sometimes through his vile belching. She harboured plans of escape, abandoning herself completely to the intoxication of hatred. "Fortunately, I didn't have any children," Marina told them. "Can you imagine a boy begotten in such moral filth and hatred? I would have brought into the world a killer, a rabid beast who would sow the seeds of violence and war upon his path, even if I surrounded him with my tenderness and my caresses, the harm would have been done, and my loving arms and my milk could never erase the curse deep in his heart. As for a daughter, I could not accept the idea of bringing into the world a little body that, as it grew, would become a piece of meat to be brutalized.

"In Saudi Arabia, we lived in grand style because of Asim's fortune. We lived in the richest neighbourhood in Riyadh, not very far from the princely palaces of the rulers. Outside the house, I usually had to wear a veil, I had no right to vote or drive a car, but in the villas and palaces, I went to orgies and sex parties that are unimaginable to us from the Balkans. I had lots of servants in the house—cooks, maids, gardeners, and chauffeurs—but I didn't really know how to give orders. I didn't know how to make them obey me, I detested the role of boss, and Asim criticized me regularly for it until he finally turned over the reins to a proper housekeeper—just in time too, the household was in chaos.

"One day, I discovered I was pregnant, and I wanted to die. Among the domestics was an Algerian nurse, Leila, who had become my friend, and who helped me get an abortion. She convinced Asim that I had had a miscarriage. I can't tell you the pain of the operation, the floods of blood, the subsequent infections, the hysterectomy they had to perform at the hospital in the following months. I can't tell you without the nightmare coming back and tormenting me again. I had to close that chapter of my youth in order to be able to begin the chapter of my liberation. Leila and I had given death, but we both felt that, as a result of that abomination, the gates of life were opening wide for me.

"Asim lost interest in me, an 'empty vessel' he said he would send away when he found a fertile woman who would give him an heir. When the time came, he would get a divorce and would let me leave with 'a fat sum of money—we have principles, madam, in my family, we have principles, we're not scoundrels!' He no longer pursued me with his lewd attentions, the doctor had advised him to forget about it, 'Your little wife is too scarred.' This is what Leila, who had a 'third ear' alert to what was whispered in the salons, reported to me. He forgot me, in a way, took me out in public for the sake of appearances and went and satisfied his voracious appetite 'with whores, who know how to have pleasure and give pleasure,' he would say, sniggering. But I had become totally indifferent, deaf to his malice. I was at peace, serene in body and heart. I told myself that one day I would be able to create a new life for myself. He gave me plenty of money, and I put some of it aside. I dreamed only of running away. Leila was in on the secret, and she went with me everywhere, so loyal and so loving was she.

"Slowly, in the course of the idle days, we made a plan. That plan gave me wings. I decided to regain my health—and, why not, my beauty. Every day, I went jogging in our private garden and then went swimming—I had my personal instructor—and had massages by a massage therapist Leila had hired by our housekeeper. Oh! What happiness, those times spent lying on a massage table after getting out of the pool, the big strong gentle hands of my Yemenite masseuse covered with essential oils, the sweet fragrances that immersed my whole body in the exotic atmosphere of Saudi Arabia, which till then had seemed so threatening to me. I said to myself, 'If I can't heal my soul, I will at least save my body from harm.'

"Every evening, I would ask Leila, who talked to me about her country, about Constantine, where she was born, and about the faraway desert her ancestors came from, 'Do you think our plan will succeed?'"

VII

MARINA'S STORY WAS INTERRUPTED by the whistling of a shell in the distance, followed by a flash in the sky over the hill to the south and, closer, it seemed, a boom deep in the earth and then a sputtering exchange of fire. Now completely awake and alert, they expected the worst, but nothing moved nearby. The silence of the night returned, open to the conversation of the stars, which no battle ever seemed to disturb.

Adila and Bosnia wanted to hear the rest of the story Marina was burning to tell. Since Adem had got them some good coffee, they decided to make some immediately. They sipped and savoured it, their hands wrapped around the warm bowls, while Marina continued.

She described to them the escape plan she and Leila had hatched, which involved Leila's lover, a Chinese man from Hong Kong who was the chauffeur for the ladies of Asim's household. Chino—that's what he was called in Riyadh, even by his lover Leila—wanted nothing more than to flee that house where the beautiful young mistress languished and the master behaved like a savage beast. Chino had had it "up to here," as he said in his rough Arabic, "up to here with the uniform and the gleaming limousine, and with this house, this city, this country of a thousand prisons and a million minarets!" Chino had long dreamed of leaving, and his mistress needed him, and his lover would come along, and they had a car—what more could he ask?

Ever since she had been a small child, Marina had dreamed of going to Djibouti, and especially to the Tadjoura coast nearby. When she was young, she had listened a hundred times to her mother telling the story of her great-aunt Alma, who, after being raped by the imam of her village, had vanished one night to escape being stoned and avoid bringing shame to the family she had dishonoured. The baker in the neighbouring village had disappeared at the same time. For years there was no news of Alma, until one day her mother, who was still alive, received a long letter from her, postmarked Tadjoura—the very name had made little Marina dream—in which she recounted her wonderful life with her baker, describing their great love and the incredible beauty of that fabulous country of a thousand and one joys. After that, Alma never wrote again. But that letter that had arrived one spring morning was read and reread at every celebration. On the slightest pretext, those yellowed pages would be taken out of their tin box, gently unfolded, and read aloud in front of the assembled family, who dreamed in unison of leaving for a land where joy finally had a name and a face, the face of Alma, who had been so pretty and who had fled this country of misery with her magician baker. That story was their family romance, a true one, and Marina had entered into that romance young, to write her own chapter one day.

Taking advantage of Asim's absence on a trip, and on the pretext of visiting the museums of Riyadh, Marina, Leila, and Chino set out one morning for Djibouti and Tadjoura. They would stay in hotels, smart hotels— before leaving, Marina had sewn her fortune into her skirts. In the car, they were as happy as children. They recited nursery rhymes and sang songs, each in his or her language—Serbo-Croatian, Arabic, and Chinese answered each other, not in cacophony, but blending into an improvised symphony based on the old music each of them remembered from childhood.

Their plan was to stay in Tadjoura for a few weeks, then go on to Herzegovina. They would go through Bab el Mandeb Strait, across the Red Sea, and through the Strait of Suez. They would stop in Alexandria and go on a little excursion on the Nile, walk arm-in-arm wearing big straw hats, and visit Chino's cousins from Hong Kong who were in business there and whom Chino hadn't seen since he was eight years old. After Egypt, they would cross the Mediterranean to Piraeus and travel north through Greece by bus as far as Macedonia, go on to Kosovo and Montenegro, and finally they would arrive home in the Bosnia-Herzegovina Marina had missed so much.

But first, Marina would spend some time in the country of Djibouti and Tadjoura, which had made at least two people so extraordinarily happy. She would first visit their graves, and then try to meet some families that would have known them. She would steep herself in the landscapes described in Alma's letter. They would go on excursions to nearby Eritrea and Ethiopia and Somalia, where she wanted to visit Cape Guardafui, where her aunt and the baker had spent their "true wedding night," as she had written in her letter.

Throughout the long journey from Riyadh to Mecca and on to Aden in Yemen, Marina, Leila, and Chino had not run into any trouble. When they stopped to eat or sleep or get gas, they encountered only friendliness and hospitality. Marina and Leila were veiled from head to foot, and with Chino as their escort and protector, no harm could come to them.

One day, returning from Addis Ababa—her aunt had described in detail the wonderful railway trips she and her lover had taken twice a year between Djibouti and that city—they had almost reached their hotel when they saw two gorillas in black suits and dark glasses getting out of a black Jaguar with tinted windows. These black crows were Asim's henchmen, who had come to get them. "It did not take us very long to understand them, they made it very clear what they wanted—but we never knew how they had managed to track us down. One of them grabbed Chino and the other one took Leila and me to our rooms and ordered us to pack our bags as quickly as possible. He paid the hotel bill.

"The return trip was non-stop, in two cars, with Leila and me in the Jaguar and Chino in his car with the second of the thugs. The return to Asim's house was just as unpleasant. I would have expected him to be violent, but he wasn't—I understood why later. I was locked up in my rooms under guard by a gigantic woman who refused to laugh or speak, and who made me undress, inspected my clothes and in a rage pulled out the sewn-in banknotes, ordered me to take a bath, which she drew steaming hot, and finally threw a tray of supper at me, a miserable prisoner's meal, which I wolfed down anyway, I was famished.

"The next day, after a black night, without stars and without dreams, I was awakened by blazing sunlight. I was surprised to find myself there in that bed I had fled with such joy. And I was astonished that I wasn't being made to suffer. Numb, my heart cold, I sat up in bed and waited for something to happen, anticipating the worst.

"I was experiencing this abrupt return like an aborted dream. Since my first abortion had been followed by a hysterectomy, I wondered if this second one would lead to a lobotomy. Nothing happened all day, except that I took my meagre meals under the malevolent stare of my guard. I racked my brain trying to imagine where Leila and Chino were. I imagined all sorts of scenarios— torture, prison, death—and each one made me shiver.

"That evening, Asim knocked on my door and burst into the room, dismissing my matron. With a panicked look I'd never seen in him, a sort of fragility that made me feel sympathetic towards him for the first time, he told me to pack my bags quickly, we had to leave Saudi Arabia for Lebanon, where he had important business.

He also told me he had had 'Leila the traitor' sent back to Algeria, her country, and had granted her the privilege of taking with her his chauffeur, her Chinese lover—he had important contacts in Algeria among the senior officers in the army, and it all had been easily arranged. 'Insh'Allah! I pity whoever employs those poisonous bastard pig snakes!'

"That very night, we took a flight to Beirut.

"In Lebanon, we again lived in grand style. I was under close surveillance day and night. Asim went about his mysterious business, continued 'going to whores,' and kept on hoping to find the pearl he would marry and who would give him an heir. He started to beat me again, on the slightest pretext, I never knew why. Then he became religious and started going to the mosque regularly, returning sombre and suspicious.

"And then the war broke out. You know the horror. I didn't understand it at all. All those political parties, all those ethnic groups, all those religions. It was civil war, with as many faces as there were clans. I had learned Arabic in Saudi Arabia, but I had trouble understanding Lebanese Arabic. The only good times were when we had to take refuge in the shelters. There I felt free, no one was spying on me. I met people, I made friends—mostly women, the men had gone off to war or were in prison or dead, like here—we spoke freely, the fear and danger took away our prejudices, our taboos. I met women who said they knew love for the first time, and other women who rejoiced at the mere thought of not being beaten when they went home, as they were in peacetime. I saw children who cried in fright and who, when things calmed down, would play and sing—and I felt the desire, unknown to me before, to bring a child into the world, combined with the inconsolable sorrow of knowing I would never be able to.

"One afternoon when Beirut seemed to be taking a nap, I suddenly heard the sound of boots in the foyer and some men I didn't recognize came in, bellowing at the top of their lungs. They asked me to take them to the living room, and then told me point blank that Asim was dead, he had been murdered—'liquidated,' they said, for some dirty business they couldn't tell me about. They told me I had six hours to pack my bags and gave me a first-class plane ticket to Sarajevo and an envelope containing an impressive wad of U.S. money, which, by the way, was stolen from me when I arrived here. These strangers said it was lucky for me that I was beautiful and knew nothing about Asim's business. They told me a driver would come and take me to the airport, adding offhandedly that I should keep our meeting a secret or else I would in turn be 'liquidated,' wherever I was.

"I never knew who killed Asim—or how or why. I realized that in wartime, there is no law and no state of law. And I realized that wars are started by hoodlums who want to be kings.

"Shortly after my return to Sarajevo, war broke out here. Would you believe it if I told you that despite my hatred of war, there is, deep down in my soul, a secret place where I love it? I'll tell you why: the first war I experienced, in Lebanon, freed me from my tormentor and the second one, here, gave me my love."

Adila and Bosnia had dozed off.

"Do you hear me, girls? I can't completely hate war. But to hell with men who make war!"

Adila opened one eye. She had just enough energy to say, "My darling, don't you think we should sleep?"

VIII

THE SKY WAS FORGET-ME-NOT BLUE, as it is some winter mornings. Without actually sleeping in, which would have been unthinkable in these times of cold and privation, the three friends still managed to linger in bed that morning. There had been so much shelling the night before that they'd had to spend part of the night in the cellar. They had no more water or wood, and hardly anything to eat. The day would be rough— it was always risky going out to replenish supplies. It had been a long time since there had been any small open-air markets. They had become much too easy targets, and besides, from day to day, the wood of the stands and the crates and other containers were burned for warmth. Not to mention the fact that most of the small merchants—bakers, butchers, grocers—were gone. Their wives were still there, of course, but they had so much to do themselves trying to track down what they needed for the survival of their children. For a long time, too, there had been no point looking for meat, eggs, butter, or milk—the cows and chickens had disappeared with the rest.

But a black market had nevertheless developed in the city, run by certain Serbs. War or no war, business would continue, legal or illegal. For their subsistence, human beings have since time immemorial exchanged goods and money—and even human bodies, through marriage or prostitution. For their survival, they began to exchange words, creating speech to communicate what they needed and inventing numbers to be able to measure the value of what they had to exchange. So the black market had quite naturally developed at the beginning of the siege of Sarajevo and the resulting scarcity. In times of extreme need, it is better to engage in clandestine trade, or even to steal, than to have to become a cannibal, to eat your friends and family to survive.

"I can't imagine eating my friends to survive. I'd rather die myself," thought Bosnia. "Even if we wage war like savages, it's still not as bad as being cannibals," she said to her friends, which shook them from their slumber. "What's this about cannibalism?" asked Adila. "Are you dreaming, are you delirious?"

But none of them had the energy to talk about it. They were hungry and thirsty. They were cold. It was harder and harder to go and get wood where it occurred naturally, in the wooded areas at the foot of the hills, because there were snipers waiting higher up with their rifles aimed down, and everything in the streets and alleys that could be demolished for fuel had been used up already, so all that was left to do was to scavenge in the gutted buildings or to sacrifice their own furniture, the legs or arms or bars of chairs or beds—"But not the table, no, never," said Adila, "we're not going to eat off the floor" (which, alas, is what they did the following winter). "And not the books," added Bosnia, determined and pensive, "books are my life. If there were no more books, I would have to write some, just so I could still read." Adila and Marina glanced knowingly at each other—where would she find the paper, poor thing?—but they said nothing, not wanting to hurt their friend, there was enough suffering in normal life. But who even knew what was normal any more? "Isn't it normal to be crazy in wartime?" asked Adila. No one said anything—to ask the question was to answer it.

Bosnia decided that after the morning's errands, she would go see her mother in the psychiatric hospital— she had not yet felt strong enough to go there—and would take some little treats for her. "Al-Lat, you the all-mothering God, let me find some treats for Mama!" And the Bach partita rose up from deep in her inner labyrinth, every note as clear as if she had written it herself, and she remembered the forget-me-not blue sky of winter that had enveloped her awakening like a big shawl. She saw at the window that this beauty was gone, that the city was covered with heavy clouds heralding a storm. "Let's hurry, we have to go out before it snows, it will be gusty, it's windy out—" Bosnia did not have time to finish her sentence when they heard loud knocking on the door. All three of them tiptoed to the door and pressed their ears to it, holding their breath. "Let me in," they heard, breathed rather than clearly spoken, and recognized Adem's voice. They opened the door and it was indeed Adem, whom they hadn't seen since that day in November when they had waited for him in vain, drinking raki. Adem, much thinner, with long dishevelled hair and beard, his arms and back laden with bags, which he dropped in the apartment as soon as the door closed; Adem, smiling at them again with the beauty of his perfect teeth—something exceptional in these times— Adem, who hugged all three of them together; Adem, whose whole body trembled and whose smiling eyes nonetheless harboured a deadly rage, a cold fury they hadn't before seen in him.

He motioned to the bags on the floor and said, "Help yourselves, it's for you," and then muttered that he wanted to sleep. Bosnia pointed him to her little metal cot and he collapsed on it, fully dressed. A moment later, they saw that he was sound asleep. His breathing seemed to come from deep in his body, as if from an abyss in which it had been pent up for days and nights. This deep yet hollow breathing, plus the smell of forest and river emanating from his body, filled the little apartment with the strangeness of open spaces glimpsed only in dreams, and Bosnia thought of her brother Mumo, her soulmate, her twin. That was how she would want the man she loved to be, wild and tender, and handsome, like Mumo, and like Adem.

Bosnia was drawn out of her daydream by the laughter of her friends. They were unpacking the bags. What treasures! In one, there were bundles of firewood, lighters, and matches; in the other, eggs, milk, bread, white beans, onions, turnips, a chunk of salt pork, and a little chocolate. Today, all they would need to get was water.

(So where had Adem found this treasure trove? When he woke up, he told them, over the dish of beans with pork that had been simmering all day, that he had just joined the Bosnian resistance army and had received these provisions from the commanding officer at the barracks.)

Adila, Bosnia, and Marina talked over their plans for the day to the rhythm of their friend's breathing, drinking hot chocolate and eating "ammunition bread," black and nutritious, which they dunked into their steaming bowls. Adila would stay home and cook the beans, and Bosnia and Marina would go out, laden with bottles and pails, in search of water—they knew all the places where rickety makeshift plumbing had been installed to connect to some supply of groundwater that the diviners had found. Later, on their way through the alleys, that morning with snow in the air and the wind gusting, they would talk about the fact that nothing could stop artists from expressing themselves, not even war. "You know," Marina would say, "in the refugee camps and safe houses, there are musicians who keep on composing—I knew one in Lebanon who played his latest works for us on the harmonica—there are writers who keep on writing, poets who still sing, and painters who even portray the beauty of the ruins. And there are still diviners who, even under the rain of shells, can hear the water flowing underground."

Bosnia searched the sky. The storm was coming. They dressed warmly, in hats, scarves, boots, and gloves. She hadn't worn her hat since last winter, and she suddenly remembered her mother knitting it in their house by the river, not far from Tuzla—her mother who wasn't crazy then. She saw again her brother and her father. She buried her face in the soft wool and breathed in the smell of her mother's hands, the smell of country soap, and stopped herself from crying because if she started again, it would go on all day, she could feel it. Then she decided to go to the psychiatric hospital another day. Madness was painful and frightening to her. She told herself she had to be careful. "In these times of turmoil, not more than one big emotion a day, if possible." She glanced over at Adem. Could she love him? Who would have imagined that in wartime you could want so much to love? She dismissed this daydream as the wind from the mountains swept away the clouds.

When she was already on the landing, she heard Adila's voice asking, "Couldn't you try to find us a piece of mutton?"

IX

BOSNIA AND MARINA had come back with the water. It was so heavy to carry up, with all the bottles in the backpacks and the pails hanging from each arm. Like beasts of burden, they climbed the five flights of stairs, bent under the weight of their load. "This is what ages you," Marina said, out of breath. "You must lose a year for each floor. That's how you end up with legs full of varicose veins and hair prematurely grey, dying little by little before you've even had a chance to really live. I'd like to leave, I'd like for all three of us to make arrangements to leave the country. But Adila would prefer to stay, she says if she has to die, she wants to die among her own, and I love Adila—leaving without Adila would be like dying myself. Before I met Adila, I had thought I would be miserable till the end of my days, I had resigned myself to inconsolable sorrow. I thought that was what life was. Then Adila came as if from beyond life to give me joy again, I can't explain how or why. It's because she was herself and I was myself. Love is so mysterious. You'll see, you too will love, little Bosnia, you will love and you will be loved."

They had put down their loads and were sitting on a step between two landings. Marina was holding Bosnia by the shoulders, stroking her jet-black hair. "You're a true little Bosniac," she said and kissed her on the cheek. She started to cry. The tears flowed freely now that she didn't have to fight anyone any more, now that she only had to fight for survival. The war Asim had waged against her body with his violence, that war no longer existed. There was the other one, waged against the body of her people, but it would end one day, she was sure of it, and the slaughterers would be punished. They had begun to hear talk, when they slipped out in search of wood, water, or food, or when they found themselves with strangers in the shelters. People were saying the international community would get involved, they were even saying the UN was on the side of the Bosnian Muslims and that the Croats themselves would become their allies. "There's every reason to hope, my little resistance fighter, every reason to hope for the end of this carnage. And then, for you, the start of a great love." Marina dried her tears, but she thought to herself that there was pleasure in weeping when you were in love.

They continued their climb. The smell of beans with onions and pork lent them wings for the rest of the way.

Adem emerged from his deep slumber in the late afternoon. He was hungry, but he wanted to wash before eating. And they had a full bottle of water put aside for him. They had all learned to wash from head to toe with barely a litre of cold water, a skill known only by the most deprived people, and one that all four of them were proud to have mastered. There were clothes hanging on a line stretched near the fireplace—with only one other bucketful, the three girls had done their washing that afternoon. The table was ready, with four simple place settings on the rough wood, and in the centre, the pot of beans with pork.

Adem told his story. Before enlisting at the barracks, he had gone to the village in Modriča where his family lived, a place he had not gone back to since he started studying law in Sarajevo three years ago. He knew that the entire region had been invaded by Serb soldiers from Doboj, aided by local Chetniks. He wanted to find his family, and he took the precaution of first going to see Dr. F., his high school history teacher, who was also a Serb, but a democrat and pacifist, and was against the proponents of "Greater Serbia racially pure and superior," as he had often said. Adem walked for days to reach the Bosna River, which he crossed at night by a very old little bridge he had often used. He knew the region like the back of his hand, he had travelled back and forth across it so often as a child with his father or his uncles, selling produce from their farm at the markets, and he had hunted small game there in the fall and fished in the spring and summer.

He took from his jacket pocket a book written by one of their people, Velibor Čolić, when he was in the Slavonski Brod refugee camp. "Read it," he said, "read these eye-witness accounts, and you'll understand better, you'll understand what I went through when I found my parents." Liliana, Dr. F.'s widow, who was a medical doctor, had given him the book. "You will be less alone, my child, when you know what others went through. The number of stories does not reduce the horror of the massacres, but it creates a healing solidarity among those who survive." She had given him information about the farm where the Serb resistance had hidden his parents. Their house and land were now occupied by a Serb family from Herzegovina. Liliana told him how her husband had been kidnapped and tortured to death. They had sent her his body three days later. She had buried him and had been mourning him ever since. She did not know why they had not done anything to her, and she probably never would.

When supper was finished and the dishes washed, the four friends silently rose and went to sit on cushions by the fire, wrapped in wool blankets. Adem wanted to talk, the three girls could feel it. He took out a pack of cigarettes and offered it to them (in the barracks, they always had them), and they all lit up. Adem continued his story amid the wreaths of smoke, his solemn words blending with the crackling of the dry wood, the macabre music of detonations from the outskirts of the city on all sides, and the yapping of lost dogs. He had slept at the doctor's house all day, and continued on his way at dusk. When he was a young boy hunting, he had learned to see in the dark and to move like a wolf, without a sound. The farm the doctor had told him about was some twenty kilometres away, east of Modriča. He needed no map or compass, as he knew the paths to take through the brush and rocks and fields of oats and wheat. He knew exactly, and felt the pleasure of being his own guide. All along the way, he experienced the joy of rediscovering the smells of his country childhood, the cut hay fragrant with the first frost, the noble rot of the fallen leaves mixed with the dried gum of the conifers, the smell of animals all around, the damp of summer's end in the underbrush, peasant smells carried by the east wind over this country he loved so much. The elation of that dark night mingled with the fear of being caught in an ambush and, especially, the worry that he would not find his family—his mother and his grandmother, his father and his father's brother, who had always lived with them, and his two little sisters, Aida and Malenka, who were ten and twelve years younger than he. The girls were so cute, he always used to pick them up and sing them songs so as not to cry with them for the sorrows of this cursed world.

At dawn he reached the farm. He hid behind a bush, watching the house and barn, checking every little detail, alert to the slightest noise. Everything seemed to be fast asleep, humans, animals, and nature itself. Nothing moved. He waited until the sun was fully risen, and then, since there was still no sign of activity, he walked slowly towards the house, intending to circle it before knocking on the door. So as not to scare them, he whistled a tune that his father used to sing when he went out to the fields. Coming around to the south side of the house, he saw—"But I can't go on," he said, "it was death itself that came to meet me ... "

His voice trembling, Adem started to speak again, "I saw the heads of my mother, my grandmother, my father, my uncle, and my two little sisters impaled on stakes between the barn and the house. Their bodies were nowhere near. Only that of the dog, gutted, lying on the ground. I saw them and I didn't die. I saw the cut-off heads of my family and I did not go mad. I didn't scream or weep. Nor did I feel the cold of my rage or plumb the depths of human baseness. I just took down each stake, gently lifted off each head and closed the eyes. I went into the house to get sheets and blankets for shrouds. I kissed each of their foreheads, each of their mouths, and I covered each of their heads with the soft shrouds. And I dug a big grave with a pick I found in the barn, and placed them in it all together. When I had filled in the grave, I lay down on it and I chanted some sacred words from my grandfathers and grandmothers, father and mother. I knew I was praying for the last time. For them, I was praying. For me, it was the last time.

"After that, I screamed. A scream that tore through my body and tore through the earth and sky. A scream that went around the world and took my soul away with it. A little later, I buried our dog Milo."

Adem asked Bosnia, "Could you pass me the cigarettes?"

X

ADEM HAD ASKED his commanding officer for two days' leave, saying he needed to see his family. When a people is under attack, the comings and goings of the members of the resistance army are not governed by the usual military laws. Everyone knew the valour and courage of the volunteer recruits, but they also knew they had duties other than those related to combat—burying their loved ones, for example, or searching through the rubble of their houses to find them. Milovan, the commander, who had been a jeweller before the attack on Sarajevo, told him, "Of course, Adem, take whatever time you need to find your folks," not knowing that his "folks" were Adila, Bosnia, and Marina—and had he known, he would have smiled, given him a pat on the shoulder, and agreed. Adem had gone to the barracks and enlisted immediately upon his return from Modriča. He could no longer envision his life without avenging his family, without killing as many as he could of those who were killing his people.

So he would spend two days with the girls, as he called them, and he would come back as often as the war permitted. He sat on the cushions on the floor, listening to his friends breathing in their sleep, and thought of Adila and Marina and their love for each other, and reflected that he had never before in his life seen love between two women—maybe it had existed, but he had never really paid attention—and thought that love was the most precious thing in the world. After the horror he had seen, the fruit of hatred displayed as trophies, the use of human beings—those most dear to him—to serve depravity and abjection, after the obscenity life had forced him to witness, the murderous evil that, like a cancer, ate life away to the core, Adem thought to himself that any sign of love between two human beings was the best thing in the world, and that after the war, if there ever was an after, this knowledge would take precedence over everything else—career, professional success, riches, everything he had dreamed of until then. Although he felt his soul had died when he had lain down and cried out his revolt on his family's grave, he was at home here. These girls had a warmth as sweet as that of the nearby hearth.

Before falling asleep, he thought of his father again and remembered the words the writer Frédéric Dard, whose books he had devoured, had spoken of his daughter who had died: "If I had known I loved her so much, I would have loved her more."

In the morning, the four of them sat around the table, warming themselves with bowls of hot coffee with milk, telling what they called "stories of before": before, when they were students, when they would go to cafés with their friends, laugh about everything and nothing, and make a thousand plans for the future; before, in another life, another time that seemed like ancient history now, though it was barely three years ago—that was why they already felt old. Adem, although hesitant, had an irrepressible need to continue his story where he had left off the night before. And he went on talking all morning.

After burying his family, after lying—he did not know how long—on the earth covering them, after crying out his revolt and his unfathomable sorrow and receiving no consolation, experiencing for the first time the great silence of the elements, the cold, heavy silence of things, without even the rustling of leaves or the whispering of grass, Adem had stood up, no longer knowing where or how to walk, feeling adrift from the world, as if he were on the edge of the earth about to fall into a void where there were no human voices—and suddenly, he had seen a scrap of life: a small grey cat. He picked up the little animal, lifted it to his neck, and heard it purring. He said "cat," his first word after death, his first word of beginning life again. He repeated "cat" and walked towards the house with it. The cat was hungry, and Adem found biscuits in the cupboard and a litre of curdled milk on a window sill. He fed the cat. Without thinking, he ate too.

He inspected the house. It was a neat, modest abode, and he clearly recognized his mother's impeccable housekeeping. There were two bedrooms with two beds in each one—he didn't want to tarry there, to breathe in their smells; he felt clearly that if he lay down on a bed with his head buried in the pillow, he would be wallowing in death, and he knew, at the precise moment when he left the bedroom with the little grey cat in the hollow of his shoulder, he knew that he definitely wanted to live. That was the first teaching of the everlasting mourning he had just begun. Before returning to the kitchen, he noticed photographs of each of them on the only dresser, including one of him in which he must have been sixteen. He saw that it was him, but no longer recognized himself. He took the photos and put them in the inside pocket of his jacket, and went through all the drawers and made a little package of what he would take with him: jewellery his mother and sisters had worn, his uncle's dagger, his grandmother's hair brooch, his father's account books. As for the big holy book, he decided to take it just for fuel on the journey back. On the other slope of death, where fate had taken him, he had no more need of what he would now call those "holy fairy tales"—his faith had gone with the scream of his soul in the dark world of catastrophe.

The little cat meowed at the door. He opened the door and let it run off. He had just buckled his backpack with all his gear when he heard the sound of a large motor. He looked out the window and saw a Serb army truck stop in front of the house. Three Chetniks got out, bottles in their hands, yelling and screaming like beasts, obviously drunk, completely dishevelled, berets crooked and boots muddy. Only their Kalashnikovs, which they held at the ready, were impeccably maintained. Adem had time to observe all the details, as he had done so many times when hunting. And, as when hunting, he moved instinctively and surely, climbing the ladder to the attic with his gear, opening the little trap door and calmly closing it again. He lay and waited. He heard them stumble through the door and sit down at the kitchen table, laughing, belching, farting, swearing, shouting insults and dirty stories. It was all there: their hatred for the "backward, savage Muslims," their victorious hunt for that race of "stupid animals," the murders, the fires, the rapes. Can humanity really be so malicious and vile, Adem asked himself—and why?

That was how he had learned of the torment those brutes had inflicted on his family. Because they were the ones who had tortured and decapitated them, as they recounted with pleasure. They had raped the four women—the grandmother, the mother, and the two little sisters—they had profaned their bodies in front of his father and uncle, who were tied up. They had impaled the heads on stakes and loaded the bodies in the truck before going for a drink in the village and throwing them in the river. That was where they were returning from. And they planned to spend the night there, to eat whatever remained and loot the house and barn and then set them on fire, before leaving in the morning for other conquests. Hearing of the rape of his grandmother, his mother, and his two little sisters Aida and Malenka in front of his father's and his uncle's horrified eyes was a second death for Adem, and being unable to throw himself upon the slaughterers as his whole body demanded, or even to weep, much less to cry out, he absorbed the teaching of that second mourning alone, motionless, soaked in cold sweat. He would now learn murder. He bided his time.

In his silent rage, he was able to carry out his plan all the more easily because the three brutes below were so drunk they could no longer even speak coherently. They belched their last slobbering stupidities through snoring that suggested they would soon be comatose. Adem waited until the three bodies slumped to the floor—they didn't even have the energy to get into the beds.

"You understand," said Adem, "my thirst for revenge was accompanied by pure survival instinct. I had to kill them when they were sound asleep, or else I was done for. I had to move quickly but carefully, because I did not want to risk waking up those pigs. First I ordered my body to stop trembling, I breathed deeply but silently, only through my nose. My Kalashnikov was dismantled, the parts wrapped in a scarf among my things in my pack, which was lying at my feet. I retrieved the pack—every moment seemed like an eternity—slid it gently along my body, unbuckled it, and took out the bundle. Being totally familiar with my weapon, I managed to assemble it in the darkness. I only had eight bullets left, but I was determined to use only three. I had hunted elk in the Black Forest in Germany, where I used to go with my mother to visit her brother. If I could take accurate aim at a moving animal, I figured it would be easy to kill the three monsters sprawled inert on the kitchen floor.

"I could hear them snoring loudly, and the stink of alcohol and piss had seeped up through the cracks in the trap door. I opened it carefully—the thunderous snoring emanating from their barrel-like bodies made it easy for me to climb down the little ladder, which luckily did not creak. Like a lynx, I was down in a flash and, like that cat I know so well, I could make out the three masses in the dim light of the moon—there were no clouds that night, I thanked heaven for that lucky break even though I no longer believed; in my heart I said a silent secular prayer, whose words I've forgotten. I slowly raised my gun to my shoulder, aiming at each of their heads. I fired one, two, three shots, and that was it, they were dead, I had killed them. I went and checked their carotid arteries, the way you do with animals, and they had really passed over to the other side of life. But unlike the hunting ritual my uncle had taught me, I did not ask their forgiveness or thank them for the meat. I would leave their vile meat there to rot. I put away my weapon, picked up my gear, and opened the door, where the little grey cat was waiting for me. Day was dawning, and the air was fresh and pure. I went by the grave of my family and said to them, 'It's done! Rest in peace. You have been avenged. I have to leave you now. I will come back after the war and give you a proper burial in the garden of our house in Modriča.' Then I threw one last clump of earth on the grave after bringing it to my lips for a kiss.

"Would you understand if I told you that, for me, the worst horror of the war was that I felt pleasure when I killed them?"

XI

"YOU UNDERSTAND, Bosnia, when I spoke of the pleasure of killing those brutes, I was not talking about enjoyment. It was rather a deadly joy, as if a triumphant ghost had got into my bones. I looked at those bodies lying on the floor, and I could see the streams of blood. They were so different from me, those three that had robbed me of my childhood and my happiness, that suddenly I was gripped by fear and cold. The murderers of my family would never do harm to anyone again, and I was relieved, proud of what I had done. I felt like spitting on them and laughing, but I didn't. You see, I wanted death—to lie once again on the grave of my family, and to die too. That pleasure I spoke of this morning was the pleasure of death."

Bosnia and Adem were walking together through the streets of Sarajevo. She had decided to go see her mother that day, and he was returning to his barracks as promised. They were holding hands. Talking. Or not talking any more, but calmed by the rhythm of their walk, these streets and alleys they were going through together, the city's silence and their own. It was as if without even saying a word, they comforted each other, as if the great sorrow each of them felt could now be healed by the presence of the other. Bosnia and Adem were two solitudes that made good company.

"I don't wish on anyone the pleasure in death that I felt," Adem continued.

Bosnia thought of her rape when she was fourteen. She saw again that uncle, her father's elder brother, that gentle, generous man, that great mystic, for whom every member of the family felt respect and admiration, who would never dream of failing to fulfill his religious duties—his five daily prayers at the mosque, his Ramadan, and his annual pilgrimage to Mecca—and she saw again for the thousandth time the indelible scene that had sowed the very death of desire in her and infected her with a desire for death. She saw him again, her saintly uncle who, one day when they were alone in the house, had turned into a devil, cynical and crazy, taken out his Koran, and shouted words from the suras mixed with obscenities. She saw him rushing at her, tearing off her clothes, throwing the Koran on the floor beside her, forcing her down on all fours, and penetrating her from behind, all the while screaming his holy verses, until she lost consciousness in tears and blood. She would never again be a child.

She remembered her mother coming back from the fields and taking her in her arms, not wanting to hear or to say a single word, giving her a hot bath, making her linden sapwood tea, massaging her body with almond oil, weeping, rocking her, singing lullabies as when she was little, and staying beside her until she fell asleep wrapped in the clean linen sheet that was reserved for the major ceremonies of life—births and deaths—with a white cotton towel between her thighs and pains in her lower belly from where the blood flowed.

She remembered, too, that when she woke up, her dear father no longer wanted to speak to her or even look at her. The uncle had disappeared. He was not seen again. In the weeks that followed, her father told her never to tell anyone this story that had dishonoured the family. He told her that she, Sabaheta, was the source of this dishonour and that it was his duty to punish her, but that he loved her too much and could not. Could not stone her. Nor whip her. Nor burn her alive. He could not. He asked God's forgiveness for this cowardice before her mother, her brother Mumo, and her; he asked for forgiveness, his hands clasped in prayer and his eyes looking to the heavens, Insh'Allah!

That did not stop the young woman from wanting to fight with him in the forest after Mumo's death and her mother's admission to the mental hospital. To join the guerrillas with him, she had cut her hair short like a boy's and worn a dagger in her belt. When he taught her how to handle a Kalashnikov, one evening after saying his prayers under the moon and the stars, he brought up the story of that rape—even uttering the taboo word *rape*—and finally, putting his arm around her shoulders and weeping hot tears on her neck, asked her forgiveness. Only that evening was she able to recover the pure vision of her childhood—a return to the past that had the power to stave off old age and death.

She had told Adem everything. She could finally tell him, who had put words to the mingling of pleasure with death, what she had until then kept silent. Adem had listened without reacting. Before the war, he had never thought about the reality of rape. He had been brought up to think that a woman who was raped was the dishonour of her family. It went without saying, no one looked further; it seemed natural to think that way, as natural as the rain that falls when the clouds burst or the night that follows day. He had never thought about the fact that some men take pleasure in causing pain, even to the point of death—and enjoying it because it causes death. He had never considered that males could use their sex as a weapon and that the bodies of women would thus become for them the equivalent of houses to be looted or territories to be conquered and defiled. These thoughts troubled him now that these women who were so close to him—his grandmother, his mother, his little sisters Aida and Malenka, and this friend Bosnia that he loved more and more without quite daring to admit it to himself—now that these women who were so dear to him had all been subjected to the ultimate torture, the supreme defilement. He saw with a feeling of nameless sadness that humanity created its own hell and he could not understand why; he felt like vomiting or throwing himself in the Miljacka River that flows to the sea like the Bosna, or else going bravely, weapon in hand, to the Dinaric Alps, that fortress between his people and the Serbs, and calmly climbing them until an enemy killed him. Then he stopped thinking about it and no longer wished for death. On the other shore of his despair, a warm hand pressed softly against his.

It was Bosnia, bringing him back to life, Bosnia who, despite all the trials of her young life, had remained fully alive, with her laughter ready at the drop of a hat or her tears that flowed naturally at every unhappiness or beauty. Adem looked at her black curls and her fiery almond eyes—she looked like an Ottoman princess, he thought. She was still smiling in spite of everything and seemed with each step to be walking toward the other slope of a sorrow she had put behind her as one does a nightmare. He had an urge to say "I love you," but was not able. There were still those images in his mind of the barely recognizable heads and faces of those who had been so dear to him, mounted on stakes against a dark, silent sky. He simply could not get words of love out of his mouth.

Spontaneously, they both headed towards the neighbourhood of Hiroshima.* They needed to sit down, to take a rest and have a smoke. In the dim light that came down through the ruins of stone and concrete, they could contemplate the harsh blue winter sky. In a way, they felt protected there—the Serbs would no longer shell this pile of rubble, it was finished but also they felt a kind of reassuring intimacy in this setting of debris and remains that was so much like them, like what they had become. The beauty they recognized in these accidental sculptures of

---

* The name given by the residents of Sarajevo to the most heavily shelled Muslim neighbourhood.

the ruins was the same beauty they found in each other: the broken flesh of their souls, in tatters and yet capable of feeling the warmth of the golden rays of the first morning of the world.

They felt good among the ruins and spoke little, their eyes following the wreaths of smoke from the two cigarettes in the cold air, their hands still clasped. "You know, Bosnia, I would like to love you. But I don't know if I'm capable of love."

"You know, Adem, it's the same for me. For a long time, I knew happiness. But I haven't now for so many months. It's as if I'd never known it."

He kissed the palm of her hand. She kissed him on both cheeks and ruffled his hair the way she used to do to Mumo when he was little. She talked to him about Mumo's disappearance. He said he would try to get information at the barracks from the men who had come there from all over.

Then Bosnia told him about her efforts to emigrate and to take her mother with her if she got better. Exile was a sweet dream, and at the same time a painful uprooting, she knew that, but the face of the dream won out. "Only Adila and Marina know, but they want to stay here. You could come, you no longer have any ties here, maybe you would more easily forget what you've been through if you went very far away?"

"Perhaps. I don't know. I can't think too much about it, the horror lies in wait for me, I feel the dizziness of the edge of the earth when the images come back to haunt me, I step into the void and I tumble to the bottom of the world—or to the top, since the earth is round."

Adem took a piece of paper out of his pocket and carefully unfolded it. "Listen, little Bosnia, this is what I scribble in the middle of the frozen nights or in the trenches. Otherwise I can't think any more:

I warm the grave
with my tears
because they are freezing inside
my loving ones
I ask time to stop
for the clocks to run backwards

I cross alone in the world
river and sea and ocean
I implore the return upstream
that it may only be a dream

I have screamed at the door of the gods
their silence struck me with dread
abandoned
with my single torment

To the end of the galaxies I fall
where there are no more shores or ground
or memories of anything before

Waters swirl all around
stars are gone with the wind
and on me fall
drops of blood"

Adem put the paper back in his pocket. He said, "This is the way that forgetting builds a nest for itself. This is my exile." Bosnia hugged him very hard, ran her hands over his face, and whispered, "I love you, Adem."

When they parted, walking slowly to their destinations, Bosnia turned around and asked Adem, who smiled slightly, "Do you have to make love to be in love?"

XII

THE COMPLEX OF RUNDOWN BUILDINGS where the mad of
all ages were crowded had a sinister look. Nearing the
entrance, on a treeless street piled with garbage, Bosnia
heard screams, then smothered mumblings and out-of-
tune singing like atonal chants. It sounded off-key.
And the smells, beginning in the entryway, were as
nauseating as those outside. This place where the mad
were put was like a kind of antechamber to Dante's
Inferno, the chamber being inside each of these sick
minds, catatonic or trembling or roaring or running to
hide under or behind tables and beds. Bosnia was
afraid, extremely afraid, even more so than under the
shelling. The horrors of war had become familiar, but
this state that was called madness felt completely alien
to her. No one, in school or anywhere else, had ever put
into words this phenomenon, the full extent of which
she was suddenly seeing today. There were dozens of
creatures who seemed stripped of their humanity there
on that bizarre stage, gesticulating or screaming with
no apparent logic, on the floor and along the walls or

clinging like monkeys to the bars on the windows through which they could not escape.

When one of them rushed towards her hopping like a kangaroo, grabbed her legs, and crawled up them with his hands, she screamed uncontrollably, and the kangaroo ran away as fast as he had come. She wanted to leave, to get out in the open air—"Even under shelling, you can breathe better than in here," she said to herself—but she remembered that her mother was here. She looked for her among those pale, distraught faces, but did not see her. A matron came towards her—she must have heard her scream—"Who are you looking for, girl?" she asked.

"My mother, I've come to see Mama."

"Can't you see you took the wrong door? There are just men here. You're lucky, they could've ripped you to shreds. What's more, these are the worst ones. Riffraff. Garbage. We put them into categories. What's your mother's name?"

Bosnia learned where the door to the women's section was, and that her mother was classified among the "lightweights." She would find her in Ward 4, at the end of the second corridor, on the left. The shrew gave a volley of lashes—to her "cattle," she said to Bosnia—and then disappeared down another corridor. Walking down the second corridor, which was quite calm, Bosnia heard sublime music coming from a glassed-in room with "Ward 1" written above the door. She recognized Bach's *Goldberg Variations*—the musician was definitely accompanying her in her filial duties—and saw at the far end of the ward a white upright piano, which an old man with long white hair was playing like a master. Bosnia felt as if she were in the middle of a dream. Here, in this menacing asylum, a white head, a white piano, and slender, ancient hands that created pure beauty—this was how she had imagined paradise when she was little! As she listened to these sounds of which the war had totally deprived her, she rediscovered the emotion of concerts—she used to go to them often, almost always with her mother, who, when she was young and living in Romania with her parents, had received an excellent musical education.

(When her mother started to speak again, she would ask her how she had met her father and whether she had loved him. And why and how she had ended up on a little farm in Bosnia-Herzegovina.)

The inspired white-haired master played all the variations. Then he gently closed the piano, stood up, put the seat back, and left the room without even noticing Bosnia, his gaze off in the distance. "He's lost in his music," thought Bosnia, "wrapped up in his music. That, at least, is a beautiful madness."

There were a lot of women in Ward 4, mostly old women but also a few young ones. A great silence fell when she entered. They all looked at her, except one, who was seated in a corner near a window, staring out blankly. It was her mother. In profile, with her hands crossed on her belly—which seemed to have doubled in size—Bosnia recognized her immediately, and she walked towards her. It was her mother Bosnia kissed, but she was like a stranger, with her vacant stare into the distance through the window. She seemed not to recognize her own daughter—not even to know she was there. Her head still held high with that posture she had always had that could seem haughty if you did not know her, her mother was there, quite present but at the same time elsewhere. Bosnia was so frightened by this situation that she thought of taking to her heels, rushing to the exit, running, running through the streets of Sarajevo, climbing the stairs in her building four at a time, and falling into the arms of Adila and Marina, who would reassure her. Or running to the barracks and asking the commanding officer to accept her as one of his fighters, and then fighting and killing those bastards down to the last one, those damned filthy Christians who had brought all the sorrow.

But Bosnia stayed. She moved a chair close to her mother's, looked into her blank, bulging eyes, and then looked no more, it was too frightening and too painful. Like her mother, she let her gaze drift to the landscape delineated by the window, and she tried to imagine a horizon that they would push back towards far-off lands where there was no war, through forests, valleys, lakes, and mountains and, why not, as far as oceans mauve under fiery sunsets. She put her arm around her mother's shoulders, pressed her head against hers, and, without even thinking, began humming a lullaby from long ago that her grandmother had sung when she was little. She no longer remembered the words, just the melody, but then some of the words came back from the recesses of memory—there was the month of May and the month of July, there were cherries and lily-of-the-valley and a fiancée coming back from a meadow with her big straw hat, a pink ribbon wafting in the gentle breeze, a fiancée going down to the river to meet her fiancé. Bosnia felt her mother's tears flowing down her own cheek, and she realized that the ward was suddenly filled with silence, a silence interrupted only by convulsive voices occasionally attempting sounds or words, a strange choir accompanying her reunion with her little old mother.

The melody of the song flowed all by itself in a series of phrases that, she hoped without really believing it, might be able to penetrate the fortress of that mind that had once been so bright and that now seemed devoid of light.

"Mama, if I didn't come to see you before, it was because I was afraid, I have always been very afraid, you know, madness terrifies me. And it was also because I needed to gather my strength, to heal from all the trials I experienced with Papa in the forest after we lost Mumo and you became sick in your mind. I don't know if you understand but I have to tell you, we've had no news of Mumo, no one has seen him anywhere. And Papa, your husband, your beloved Ismet, is dead. I want you to know he was brave right to the end. He defended us valiantly, but one day when I was coming back from hunting rabbits, I found him lifeless. He'd been murdered. His body was still warm. I closed his eyes, chanted all the prayers I could for him, and I told him I would see to your welfare—I didn't say your happiness because nobody here knows what happiness is any more. I dug him a grave in the earth and I stayed with him for a long time. But, you understand, I had to leave him there so that I wouldn't die too. It took me days getting out of the woods. The guerrilla group would have been too dangerous for me all alone. I'm in Sarajevo now, in the apartment I lived in as a student, with Adila, whom you know, and a friend named Marina. We get along well together, we're surviving. The war goes on, you know. The Serbs are enraged and want to eliminate us. But we are resisting. We now have a Bosnian army that is fighting, and the Croats are on our side. And it seems the international community will come and help us.

"The war goes on and I'm careful. I want to live, you know. I'll come back and see you as often as I can. I've brought you an apple and some little treats. A friend, Adem, who signed up at the barracks, gave them to me for you. I want to tell you I love Adem, and it's the first time in my life that I know this state of joy. And to tell you that, in the forest, Papa asked my forgiveness for what happened with the rape, you remember. He even said the word, and he cried. One day I'll come and see you with Adem.

"And if you want, if you get better, one day we'll leave together for a country that lives in peace. I'm making arrangements. I'll talk to you about it again. But you have to get better, little Mama. Other countries don't want to take in refugees who are sick in body or mind. Tell me, Mama, are you going to get better?"

XIII

THEY HAD TO FACE IT, there was no more wood. Winter continued with its cold, it was endless, and there was no more wood. They could still find water in the makeshift taps, and although food was scarce too, they always managed to find some itinerant merchant in the clandestine invisible bazaars in the basements close to the water sources. They had very little to eat, of course, and they went without what in time of peace seemed essential—eggs, milk, butter, meat, and fish—but they got by, they survived. Wood was another matter, there was simply no more to be had. No more window frames or wood thresholds or doors, no carts or wagons, no shovel, mop, or rake handles, and no more furniture—they had burned it all. They had given up the daily mourning ceremonies that used to take place—in the beginning, some people would kiss the everyday objects, some of them, always women, would even cry, but then they learned to throw them indifferently into the fire that would consume them, the way they'd roast chestnuts or stoke bonfires in the old life. Finally, the worst horror of the war was that you ended up taking for granted the destruction of beloved beings and things, living with death as if it were a constant part of normal everyday life.

There was so little wood that the seven hills had become bald, except for the summits that the snipers had kept for themselves so they could shoot without being flushed out. Bosnia noticed one day that, shaven like that, the seven hills looked like heads of the Iroquois of the St. Lawrence and the Susquehanna, and that when the light was dim, her city seemed surrounded by giant, threatening Mohawks like those she had seen as a teenager in a book on the history of the Americas. No one could take the risk any more of going out in the open on the now-bare slopes of the hills, and the bodies that had fallen there and been buried as quickly as possible, with little stones or blocks of concrete to mark their presence, had replaced the trees and bushes that had once made summer in Sarajevo so beautiful. Sarajevo had become an old woman who had mourned too many dead, her beauty vanished, recognized only by a few familiars and lovers from fragile clues.

Wood was rare and the few sticks discovered by the armed soldiers now stayed at the front, that is, in the barracks. After all, they had been defending the besieged city for so long, they had to stay warm and to eat and sleep a little before spreading out in the trenches that were dug almost everywhere, industrious little ants, barely visible, that an enemy boot would crush from time to time.

There was no more wood and the three girls, Adila, Bosnia, and Marina, would have to face the worst if they did not want to perish as statues of ice that would melt in the spring. They would have to burn the books! Everything else in the apartment was gone: chairs and little tables, the kitchen table, the bed, shelves, cupboard doors, and even old clothes. It had all been used to feed the fire since excursions to the outskirts of Sarajevo had become too risky, and since the fighters had started keeping all the precious wood for themselves. It was with a lump in his throat and a heavy heart that Adem had informed them of his commander's decision.

They therefore held a war council that afternoon, on which books they should get rid of first and which ones they should keep until the very end. They had spent the morning in the basement, because the shelling had not stopped since dawn. There were eight of them in the shelter, women and children—the old man who was usually with them had died alone in his apartment, no one really knew of what, a neighbour who went in every day to look after him had found him one morning—and one of the women in the group, a sturdy peasant who had come from Visegrad* at the very beginning of the war, invited them all to come to her place for spit-roasted pigeon and potatoes baked on charcoal when the alert was over. They were coming back from there, bellies full and cheeks red, their hostess the Gypsy—that's what everybody in the building called her, and no one knew anything about her life—having served with her pigeon and potatoes a

---

* Visegrad has been part of the Bosnian Serb Republic (Republika Srpska) since the Dayton Agreement in 1995.

kind of wine that seemed to be made of raspberries mixed with spruce, which had gone down like lightning and warmed them up and made their heads spin. Returning home, three comical characters holding on to each other's shoulders and singing on the stairs, they had quickly come back to the reality of the cold room. They had drunk large glasses of water, fed the fire with their last scraps of wood, the remains of a shelf roughly chopped up, along with a few old socks, and, sitting on a bed wrapped up together in one big wool blanket to retain heat, they held their war council on the books.

They divided the books into three categories, the first of which consisted of the ones they could sacrifice immediately, although it was still painful: all their textbooks—"We'll get new ones when our children go to school," Adila had said, deadpan—as well as grammar books, history and geography books, books on mathematics, chemistry, botany, and physics, and even books on medicine, bought by Adila for her midwifery studies—"It breaks my heart, but we have no choice," she said in a dignified, heroic tone of voice. They put these books in the first pile, warmed up a little by the activity, and kissed the first book to be thrown on the pyre, a grammar book, alas—"But when will we go back to grammar?" Marina had asked.

After the first pile had been burned, next would go the literature, from Bosnia-Herzegovina, Yugoslavia, Europe, and the world, books in six languages that had been accumulated by Adila and Bosnia, a treasure they had added to over the years. But it was Bosnia, the great reader, as they called her, who had to make the biggest sacrifice—books she had found here and there in sales or received as gifts since childhood—and Bosnia who in a firm, distant tone of voice tried not to show her pain but who told them, "These ones I don't even want to touch, put them in piles and burn them when I'm not here," and went to get the novels of Giono and Dostoyevsky that she had hidden under her mattress, and the two friends pretended not to see. Finally, in the very last category, they put the dictionaries (Serbo-Croatian, but also others in several European languages), which also belonged to Bosnia.

And the Koran? There was no question of burning the great holy book. "That, never!" they had cried. It would have been a sacrilege. And dangerous. Without being great believers, such a profanation, such an act of impiety and blasphemy, especially by fire, raised the prospect of eternal damnation in hell. No, not the Koran! "And not the Bible," Marina had added, because there was a pocket Bible on the bookshelf, given to her by her Catholic Croat father when she was little, that she had always kept as a talisman, unbeknownst to her Muslim maternal family or to Asim, her deceased tormentor. "Not my little Bible either," insisted Marina. "On my father's side, our holy book is the New Testament, we are descended from Jesus Christ and the Apostles, and from Mary, Elizabeth, Anne, and Mary Magdalene, that is our age-old lineage."

Watching the books being consumed, all those letters going up in smoke, the three friends nibbled on dry bread and sipped cups of hot chicory—they had not been able to find coffee for weeks—and started talking about the existence of God and their beliefs. For Adila, who still wore a headscarf when she went out, the faith of her childhood did not cause any problems, and besides, "I hardly ever think about it. I was not interested in the big metaphysical questions in school, and am even less so since the disaster of the war. God, for me, is in the bodies to be nursed, the children to be brought into the world, the wounds to be bandaged, the water I fetch every day, the suffering I comfort all around me, Insh'Allah."

Marina, the eldest of the three, the beauty with golden hair and sea-green eyes, who had known her share of pain and who seemed sometimes to have got over everything, declared, "For me, I can tell you, it's simple, I don't believe in anything any more, neither Allah nor God nor Mohammed, and not even Jesus Christ, although I told you I was descended from him by the paternal line, which is the absolute truth. I won't believe in anything or anyone any more, as long as this world is run by bloodthirsty tyrants, rapists, and thieves, creators of carnage and merchants of torture devices, I will no longer believe in anything or anyone as long as evil rules this world of catastrophe and corruption. To me, it's simple, if God/Allah really existed, goodness would govern the world because if God/Allah is not good, He can't be the Supreme Being. For me, wearing the veil is only an effect of the commandments of perverted males who see women's sex on their heads, and I'd even say—I've had time to think about it, all alone in Saudi Arabia and Lebanon—

that their perversity is double: with the veil, it's the sex on our heads that we are supposed to conceal, but it's really our heads that we have to hide, it's our ability to think. Outside, the heads and thoughts of women are kept in the dark. Inside, in the secrecy of the home, true sex is given over to their voracious obscenities. I've thought a lot about it, you know. All their holy yarns to keep us subjugated to their fornicating desires—no thank you! I want to live. With Adila, I have known love that does not cause pain. Love is what is good between two people. That's all. You can wear the veil outside, my dear Adila, I respect your beliefs. But for me, basta!"

Adila kissed Marina, crying, "I don't know why I'm crying, it's the war, these books that are burning, Allah, Jesus Christ, the beatings, the rapes—everything is so complicated—I love you ... "

Bosnia said, almost in a whisper, "If God were a woman, if She were all goodness, all mercy, Al-Lat, then I would believe. I've been wearing the scarf since I made the promise to my father when I buried his body, but I don't know why." And throwing another book on the blaze, she added, "Don't you think we should go out for water?"

XIV

BOSNIA WAS COMING BACK to her neighbourhood by way of an alley that ran parallel to "Sniper Alley,"* which she would never venture out on. She was walking in the sun, her whole delighted body soaking up its warmth. Finally, spring was back. Would happiness come back with the mild weather and beckon to her once again? She hardly believed in it any more, but she had seen its tracks these recent weeks—in Adem, whose presence was pure joy for her; in her mother, whom she had just left and with whom she had been able to walk a little outdoors, who seemed to be doing better and who had even smiled slightly while watching a flock of storks pass, leaving in their wake as they headed towards the Baltic the fragrances of far-off Africa and the Mediterranean; and in her dear Adila and Marina, who, through the sheer magic of friendship, had transformed

---

* So named by the residents of Sarajevo, this open avenue was the site of daily shootings during the siege of the city, and many people were killed there.

the tormented life that had been hers for so long into relative peace.

She felt the sun warming the ravaged stones, inhaled the perfume of the buds bursting with their scents, and watched the frost melting on the windows, trickling down in an infinity of designs—all kinds of animal and human faces, shapes familiar or fanciful as those in the fleeting museum of the clouds—she heard the dozens of little streams from the melting snow, in which she skipped as in childhood, light, almost weightless, with that feeling of pure nostalgia in her heart that comes when a time that seemed lost forever returns like an old companion, at once remote and present, bringing both tears and laughter.

"What will I do with the precise memory of spring returning, of this afternoon when it seems as if the war has gone, after I've become a refugee in another country? Will I be able to experience elsewhere what I have here today? And how?"

Bosnia was not very far from her building when, in a fraction of a second, everything was turned upside-down: there was the dull thud of a shell not far away, then shattering glass, a rain of broken concrete and stones all around, a streak of earth in the blowing black smoke, screams, frightened footsteps running every which way, howling and yapping—then nothing, the numbing silence of death punctuated with groans and, here and there, the wings of pigeons fleeing. Frozen to the spot, Bosnia waited where she had taken refuge, her back against a wall in the shadow cast by a disused building in the bright mid-afternoon sunshine, she found herself numb in the darkness and damp, she felt nothing, immobilized and holding her breath, she was waiting. Waiting for what? She did not know exactly— the shelling had anaesthetized her whole body and her thoughts within. Soon, she heard cautious footsteps on the other side of the stone wall, on what she knew was her street, heading east toward her building. After waiting a little longer, she crossed through the abandoned building, a shortcut she had often taken, and was back on her street, which was flooded with sunshine and strewn with debris and bodies and parts of bodies. The living were beginning to come out of the shelters, walking among the dead as in a slow-motion film. Bosnia saw them bend over the field of human ruins, moving bodies, sometimes putting heads and arms back in their places, all of them silent, without cries, without words, women, mostly, and old men and children, thrown onto an apocalyptic stage where their role was to perform these movements of human shadows in the slow procession accompanying their loved ones to the inhuman kingdom of shadows.

They lined up the bodies—whole or dismembered— in the courtyard of a little house that had been shelled in the early days of the war, in a rectangle where a little wild garden had formed within the broken walls—you could even see the first snow-drops and daffodils shining there like tiny funeral lamps. They placed all these envelopes of consumed flesh here for burial—it had been months since anyone had gone to the cemeteries, those former places of eternal rest had become territories of mortal danger, so it was here that they would in the coming hours improvise a collective funeral ceremony, like the ones that had been performed so many times, now that death, like life, had become their infernal companion. Out of respect for tradition, they would dig deeper holes in the earth for the women, and since there were more women here, they would have to spend a lot of time digging. One of the older women would be chosen to be the *bula*, she would veil herself for the occasion and sing hymns so sad that there would remain in the hearts of the mourners, until the end of their days, sharp splinters that no joy could ever remove.

Bosnia moved towards the macabre scene as if in a bad dream, looking everywhere for her friends, who must have taken refuge in a shelter, since their building had been hit. Suddenly, the unthinkable, intolerable sight—on the ground, the bodies of two women, still holding hands—then a scream rending the air, the scream of Bosnia looking at her dead friends Adila and Marina, and then Bosnia seeing nothing more, Bosnia totally in her scream, in her vision of a world of absolute blackness, of an earth that had split open to swallow her, engulfing all three of them, Bosnia yelling "No!", a No that echoed off the seven hills of Sarajevo to burst the eardrums of the sadistic gunners up there, and came back in shreds to the weary gravediggers in the wild garden, a No that reverberated like a bomb in the ears of the small crowd of women and children and old men, a sorrowful group created by an accident of human history, a silent multitude bending under its deathly task, a sum of solitudes cut through by a single repeated cry, the cry of Bosnia staring at the bodies of the dead friends she loved so much.

(She would learn later that her two friends were coming back from their daily errands when the shell hit their building. Like the others in the neighbourhood who were killed that day, they did not have time to run to a shelter.)

But right now, Bosnia was not thinking, no information could reach her. She was in the indescribable. She was in the unimaginable. She was in her blind vision of the two bodies of her dead friends stretched out on the ground. She was in her No. Her whole body was in refusal. She was in her cry.

And then she felt an arm around her shoulders and she heard words she would repeat to herself often until the end of her days, she heard them because they were spoken by the man she loved, Adem, and her cry would stop to allow them to resonate and reach her inner labyrinth: "Little sister, little Bosnia, after the ceremony, I'm taking you to the barracks. Come with me. I've asked the commander. I don't want to abandon you, ever. We'll make arrangements together to get out of here. We'll go live elsewhere. Far away. Wherever you want. We'll take your mother with us when she's better. Little sister Bosnia, I love you."

(It was the Gypsy who had run breathlessly to the barracks to look for Adem, knowing he was the only one who could be of comfort to her young neighbour in this situation.)

When Bosnia heard "I love you," she imagined that place elsewhere to which the two of them would move away with her mother. She again saw her two friends, and then she looked at Adem and saw his eyes travel to the other side of the horizon of death. Her cry had died out with Adem's first words. She let rise from the unfathomable abyss of her earth—her heart, belly, guts—a long sob, a flood of mingled salt and blood, muffled in the hollow of Adem's shoulder, a deep intimate moan accompanied by the incantations of the *bula* and the cawing of a crow perched on the highest branch of a charred chestnut tree.

Before burying the bodies of their friends in a single grave, pressed close to each other as they had lived and as they had died, Bosnia used Adila's veil to make her shroud, and taking off the scarf she had worn since the burial of her father, she covered Marina's body with it. She said, and only Adem understood, "Forgive me, Papa. I promised on your grave to wear this scarf. On the grave of my friends, I am freeing myself from that promise." In Adem's car, she added, "Neither God nor Devil. I am free. No more of that."

Leaving the makeshift cemetery, leaving behind them the little crowd of mourners, some in tears, others meditative, but all angry, Bosnia and Adem stopped not far from their friends' common grave, to contemplate a yellow primrose glowing in the face of the world like a ray of sunshine lighting up a tiny part of that dark night in besieged Sarajevo.

Adem took Bosnia's hand and said simply, "Are you coming with me?"

XV

IN THE BARRACKS, Milovan, the commander, had had a dormitory set up near the kitchens for the few women who had ended up there—mothers or sisters of soldiers, and orphan girls who had lost everything and did not want to find themselves in Serb bordellos. One of them had become a soldier, the rest cooked or cleaned, and the youngest, who were still children, did light chores. Milovan felt that when Bosnia recovered from the state of prostration she had been in since her friends' deaths, she would make an excellent teacher for the little girls and the three or four young boys, orphans picked up here and there in the city, who were too small to handle weapons and who, like the girls, often spent the night crying over their parents' deaths. Milovan had been thinking that a school would do a lot of good for this lonely, idle brood. But the women in the barracks were more or less illiterate, so Bosnia's arrival was a real gift from heaven—particularly in these accursed times when all that came from above was thunder and punishment, Insh'Allah.

Milovan was waiting for Bosnia to get better in order to set up the school. He also knew that Bosnia would likely want to fight alongside his men and her brave Adem—she had proven herself capable with the guerrillas—but the school would only take three hours a day, so she would be free to fight the rest of the time. She was gorgeous, this young girl with her wild beauty, and these courageous, spirited, sometimes reckless, young people, boys and girls, that the war had revealed to him were so admirable to Milovan, who had never had a wife or children, and had known few of his people other than those who came from time to time into the back room of his shop in the big bazaar to have their watches repaired or to buy jewellery. The war had awakened a dormant paternal instinct in him, and he considered these young fighters, many of them orphans, his own family. When one of them fell, cut down in combat, he was deeply affected, every loss was for him a mourning for this strange family the war had given him. But whenever there was serious misconduct on the part of one of the boys, such as that matter of the rape of young women prisoners he had recently become aware of, Milovan himself felt wronged—and the punishment he meted out as head of the family was in keeping with the offence. The commander felt responsible for these armed young people who in this lawless time of war sometimes no longer knew the difference between right and wrong.

(In Milovan's barracks, there were not only classes on the art of war, there were also regular times for prayer, Allah Akbar, lessons on ethics, and when necessary, public trials in which the guilty were condemned and punished in accordance with their crimes. Soon, dreamed Milovan the jeweller turned military commander, there would be a school. If the war continued, he would have a mosque built in the courtyard of the barracks—but without a minaret, for it would be too risky, one mustn't go overboard.)

As for Bosnia, she shivered in her little bed, no longer thinking and hardly eating, existing in the half-tones of an endless day merged with night, her being floating in an in-between world, half dream, half reality, an arid desert cut off from the oasis of tears. Her whole body had fled to a region of torpor and lassitude, from which only Adem's visits could rouse her to some degree, because her love for Adem was the only little flame still alight in her life.

One afternoon of fine rain falling straight down through a steamy curtain of slanting rays, when Bosnia's ears were focused on the raindrops on the tile roof and her eyes on the window, she began to feel a slight warmth rising again from the depths of her body. She slowly closed her eyes again, and, to the rhythm of the raindrops, she took the most beautiful journey of her life. First there were the haunting words of Velibor Čolić, "I walk under the rain warm as camomile tea and I search for you," punctuating her first steps beyond the borders. Then the three girls, Adila, Bosnia, and Marina, riding three magnificent purebred criollo roans, galloped to the border of Bosnia-Herzegovina to the rhythm of the words: "I walk under the rain warm as camomile tea and I search for you." In the distance, across the Adriatic, was the smiling face of Mumo, who was waiting for them, and on the way, at the edge of the city, Bosnia had Adem climb on behind her, after spotting him walking on the sandy ground with his gun slung across his shoulder, bent under the weight of a knapsack filled to the brim, his curly black hair all dusty. Then, a little farther, her mother, who was now called Mamouni, was signalling to them with her thumb raised like a hitchhiker, and she climbed up behind Adila and held on to her by the waist.

The three criollos with their five riders moved briskly, Adila's veil floating in the wind like the sail of a boat, Marina's blonde hair mingling with her horse's auburn mane. They were laughing, shouting, singing to the words echoing from all four directions, "I walk under the rain warm as camomile tea and I search for you," the short sentence that for Bosnia represented the promise of the return of happiness, of a paradise she had believed forever lost.

They crossed all of Bosnia at full gallop, and then Croatia, southern Slovenia, northern Italy—the Alps were no obstacle to their horses—to end up in southern Provence, on the Mediterranean. "The hours consist of a great dream where silver waters dance," Bosnia said to herself, remembering Giono. The criollos, now at a trot, continued as far as the first waves, let their five riders dismount, and shook themselves in the salty foam. Bosnia recalled a book of sacred legends from her adolescence, saying the horse was created by Allah from a fistful of wind and was made king of all the domestic animals, which is why horses love to move and why they worship the wind.

Mother Mamouni, who had escaped from the asylum just to undertake this saving journey, was the first one to dismount, to embrace her horse and thank the wind, the first one to take off her shoes and hike up her skirt to walk into the water, greeting the sky as blue as the water with a cry of joy. The others, following her, threw shoes and clothes on the sand and ran half-naked into the waves, where they played and swam in their newfound freedom, washed their bodies of the filth of this world, and frolicked until nightfall.

Her face drenched in salty water, still smelling the horses and the iodine of the sea, Bosnia awoke, her body aching—she had swum for hours in the surf—and through those blessed tears, she saw Adem's face for the first time since the deaths of her friends, she saw him clearly and felt him covering her hands and her forehead with little kisses, and she said, "Allah created the sacred horse from a fistful of wind. We must respect it." She added, "I believe happiness is still possible." Adem was mystified by the sudden resurrection of his beloved. He had come to tell her that their efforts with Avocats sans Frontières would soon bear fruit and that they would be able to choose among three or four countries—Germany, England, France, and Sweden. She was to pick the best. There were piles of documents to go through. The commander knew about it and would help them financially. "You're my two children," Milovan had declared solemnly.

"Little sister Bosnia, spontaneously, which country would you choose first?"

Part Two

FRANCE

XVI

THERE IT WAS, that much imagined France, streaming past her eyes while Adem slept at her side. There it was, as in her daydreams, but the journey was showing her an unknown face, one made up of grey landscapes she had rarely seen in her books. And those books, as well loved and as true as they were, had not been written by refugees who had left behind them devastated lands, scorched earth covered with murdered bodies, who had abandoned their whole childhood, scraps of which would come back only as fleeting recollections that vanished like the rain on the wind-swept windows of the train.

There it was, and she hardly believed it, the last hours had so quickly swallowed up a whole part of her life, with no time to think, to take stock, to measure the meaning of such a departure in their lives. In each of their lives and in their life together—she and Adem loved each other and had forever joined their destinies "for better or for worse," as Milovan had said at the improvised wedding ceremony in the barracks, surrounded by witnesses from among their companions in misfortune, with the holy book, despite the fact that they no longer believed in it and Milovan knew nothing about it, the book on which they had pronounced the words of fidelity, although both their minds had flown far away from everything those words had represented for their parents. Their individual lives were now entwined and the first chapter of their life together was this train journey, full speed ahead, in this life that they were beginning to cherish since they were sharing it, they loved each other so much.

There it was, the France of their dreams streaming by now, the Rhône River, from Geneva, where they had landed, to Lyon and Adem's cousin Mirsad, whom Adem had only seen in a photograph at their grandparents' house. There it was, that France she had dreamed of in books, and as Bosnia approached it full speed ahead, her Bosnia-Herzegovina vanished, disappearing behind her, as if crossing the space was cheating time. Because time had hardly moved, only yesterday they were still in Sarajevo climbing into the Médecins du Monde truck that had taken them across the whole country, then across Croatia to Ljubljana, in Slovenia, where they had taken the plane for Geneva.

The time of yesterday was still very present, while crossing the space was taking her light-years away. Bosnia felt a kind of warping of categories, a tearing of the elements, and she thought that this paradoxical state was the first emotion of wandering, probably her first pain as a refugee. She reflected that with their meagre baggage, she and Adem were bringing the seeds of melancholy and, certainly, vestiges of anger and violence to this new country where there was peace, because she already resented the France she had held dear since her earliest youth, when reading had formed her feelings and thoughts, for so quickly robbing her of the images of her homeland.

After the mountains, the rain stopped. Bosnia needed only to follow the Rhône now, to wash away in its waters her first feeling of sadness at being uprooted. She let the movement of the train rock her and took Adem's warm hand in hers and watched him sleep. At least Adem was right there with her, rushing towards the unknown, and leaving their country of disasters and ancient wonders, at least her beloved Adem was sleeping by her side. Bosnia closed her eyes and imagined a bedroom, a bed for them alone where they could finally have their fill of loving one another; as the train rushed ahead faster than the river, she wanted Adem desperately. She gave him a little kiss on the neck and covered their two bodies with the little woollen blanket given them by a midwife with Médecins du Monde, whose name was Anne and who was from Belgium. Half dozing, she saw her mother, now named Mamouni as in her dream about the criollo horses, her Mamouni, who had left the psychiatric hospital, having recovered at the end of the hostilities and the arrival in Bosnia of the UNPROFOR* troops. Milovan had found her lodging with one of the women from the barracks, also a widow, in a squatted apartment downtown that had belonged to some Serbs who, like others, had fled to the Republika Srpska. Mamouni did not want to

---

* United Nations Protection Force.

leave her country and she had said, because she was able to talk again, "Come back and see me often, little Sabaheta. Go start a new life with Adem, you're young. At my age, you know, the roots are too deep in the earth. And my roots will entwine around your father's bones. Those who uproot the old by force are guilty of infamy, of betrayal, Allah Akbar! Come back and see me often, little Sabaheta. Write to me."

And she had left her Mamouni out of love. Sometimes leaving someone is a gift, a present given in silent ardour to a loved one. When she had kissed her on the doorstep of the bare little squatted apartment, had seen her surrounded by furniture and things that were not hers, with her hair pulled back in a bun, a blue apron tied around her waist, and big slippers on her feet, Bosnia had not wanted to cry or to turn back. Going down the stairs of the building, she had seen the warm sunbeams of August pouring in through the broken window panes, creating abstract paintings on the walls, and heard her mother say a gentle prayer, "Take care of yourself, be careful, Insh'Allah." She had heard herself shout back up the stairwell, "I'll come back and see you often. I'll write." She knew that, to her last breath, she would hold it in that most precious box in her heart's memory where the bodies of her father and her dear friends Adila and Marina were sealed; she knew it at that precise moment when their words had floated on the moving paintings of the August sun, she knew she would keep within her always that image of her mother with her blue apron, her bun, her slippers, and that imploring voice.

Tossed about by the movement of the rickety old train, her eyes fixed on the branches and grasses that looked like a thousand hands waving to greet their passing, Bosnia tried to sleep, knowing that sleep wouldn't come, being accustomed since the first fury of the war to insomnia interspersed with recollections and waking dreams. But she did not want to dwell on memories; she had submitted herself to the duty of forgetting in order to survive. So she appealed to the future and threw herself into endless scenarios of which she was the heroine—when you've come out of hell, it is hard to imagine a happy fate other than your own. Either she would become a doctor, a doctor of the mind if possible, and travel the world with Adem, who would be a lawyer without borders, helping people who were living under dictatorship and barbarism, or else she would become a painter, since it seemed to her that only paintings could express the hidden underside of words and of the horrors she had known, and that it could perhaps give back to her and to the world a little of the happiness that had gone away on the other slope of words. But, in any case, she would bring a child into the world, maybe two, maybe three, whose father would be her beloved Adem.

She watched Adem sleeping. Like a child, exactly. But sometimes the movements of his face and the contractions of his body suggested he was in the middle of a nightmare. She would gently wake him. He was never able to recount his dream. A wordless death. Nor was he able to cry. Bosnia then remembered a sentence from Julien Gracq that she had read just before the war:

"He felt beating within him a tiny desperate flutter that was like the edge of tears."* Yes, Adem was on the edge of everything. On the edge of tears. On the edge of despair. And even on the edge of love.

When they made love in the little bedroom overlooking a garden where they had lived for the last weeks—in the home of Milovan, with whom they had finally left the barracks, which had been turned over to the soldiers of SFOR,** the home of that commander they now thought of as their father and who had given them shelter and money—when their bodies were finally given totally to each other, entwined and covered with kisses, their lovemaking accompanied by the birds come back from who knows where, when Bosnia opened up like a ripe fruit to pleasure, Adem would suddenly withdraw, no longer able to ejaculate or even to grieve for the pain his impotence inflicted on the body of his "warm, tender beloved," as he would whisper in Bosnia's ear along with disjointed snatches of the images that haunted him and constantly kept him on the edge of pleasure. He said he sometimes wished he could plunge into that underground torrent with a body that would contain all the blessed liquid of sperm or tears, plunge in and drown himself, swallowing the torrential waters and putting an end once and for all to the images of his loved ones mounted on stakes against the sky and the images of the three enemies he had killed with his own

---

* From *Un balcon en forêt*.
** The NATO-led Stabilization Force for Bosnia-Herzegovina.

hands lying on the floor. Leaving Bosnia on the brink of orgasm, he would say only that he no longer wanted to look at the face of death, the face he had seen with his own disbelieving eyes. He said he wished he had never given death. Then he would fall asleep exhausted, and return to the darkness of his nightmares. Bosnia, her head on his sturdy young chest, would cry for both of them, stroking his hair and his face, overcome by a strange vertigo, her body facing the abyss of an aborted promise, like a ripe fruit that is not picked and falls to the ground, shrivelled by the first frost.

Tears flowed down her cheeks, and she emerged from her half-asleep state and saw that night had replaced dusk and that she could no longer even guess at the landscape—the first sign that one is in an unknown country. Realizing that simple, obvious fact, she felt very cold, but looking up at the sky to the east, in the direction of her country, she saw the moon, which had not changed, the moon and its stars still the same even though the constellations were not in the same places. She thanked the moon and the stars and the sky for accompanying her, constant and reassuring, on her uncertain wanderings.

The train slowed down and crossed a bridge over the Rhône, and the lights of a city that appeared huge came toward her. She saw a very large station with the letters of a name she had seen only in books— "LYON"—and further along, in smaller letters, "SNCF." She shook Adem, who emerged fresh from his own voyage, kissed her, shook himself like a puppy, and asked, "Where are we?"

XVII

THE SCREAMS AND SOBS of Sophie, the young French wife of cousin Mirsad, woke them in the morning. The screams and sobs, and Mirsad's hoarse breathing and the dull thuds of his blows in the bedroom next door. Bosnia, in shock, trembling, took refuge in Adem's arms, and he scarcely breathed, listening intently as if he was trying to understand this new form of combat that was taking place in the bedroom of the cousin he had met only the day before. Mirsad and Sophie had come to meet them at the station, and Mirsad had driven them in a rattling old jalopy to this miserable apartment in a suburb of Lyon. They had drunk beer and eaten bread and ham and had said their goodnights, a little tipsy.

While the blows were raining down, a frigid rain was beating against the window, a sinister concert from the cold outside accompanying the racket inside. Suddenly, Bosnia was no longer trembling. She sat up very straight in bed and put both feet on the floor in a fighting stance. Without premeditation, she let out a cry from her guts, a ringing "No!" that shook the walls, and then a flood of words directed at Mirsad, whom she barely knew: "Stop your blows, there's no more torture, the war is over! Stop it! In France, there is peace!" (In her mind, she was calling Mirsad a pig, a bastard, a pimp, a Chetnik, an Ustachi, a scumbag, but she did not say those words.) She looked at Adem, who had also leapt out of bed, and he gave her an approving wink and hugged her. The cousin's little apartment suddenly went completely silent, as if a black, frozen night had fallen in the middle of the morning. Nothing moved. It was as if the two in the bedroom had been turned into pillars of salt or pulverized and blown away to distant galaxies by Bosnia's words. Mirsad was no longer hitting. Sophie was no longer crying.

In the dull silence punctuated by the staccato beat of the rain, like thirty-second notes, against the windows, all the ghosts of the war passed before Adem and Bosnia. Mechanically, they walked over to the window, still holding each other, to look out at the city, and at the country that had promised them peace.

The scene outlined by the frame of the window was monotonous—no sea or mountains or forests, or even any horizon, everything was blocked by slabs of identical grey buildings lined up one after the other, each holding dozens of human cages. And they themselves were in one of the cages. They sought the sun and the water of the river, but were answered only by clouds driven east by the wind—or they assumed it was east, because that wind must be the *tramontane*. "You can't tell which direction is which with all those slabs," said Adem, and Bosnia, her nose pressed to the window streaked with rain, said, "I don't want to stay here, Adem, there's war inside the house, and from the outside, we're in prison. I want to see the river and the sea and the mountains of Roussillon and Vaucluse, I want to see the Mediterranean, I want to see Mont d'Or from Manosque, and the Alps on the horizon. Come on, let's have a coffee, Adem. We'll talk to your cousin. Sophie can come with us, we'll take her with us. Come, Adem, we'll make plans in the kitchen."

Adem was packing their bags. He too wanted to leave as quickly as possible, even if it meant sleeping at the Bosnian refugee centre Milovan had told him about. But there were also some other things he wanted to do, which he shared with Bosnia. He wanted to call Milovan and talk to him about his brother in Paris. And especially, he wanted to go to the centre in Lyon and see the people in charge of dealing with Bosnian refugees. As well, he wanted to call the lawyer from the group Avocats sans Frontières whose name and number he had been given.

They heard noises from the bedroom. Quiet voices, soft footsteps. The two statues had begun to move again. Then, the sound of water running, the front door opening and closing. From the kitchenette came the aroma of coffee, mellow and tantalizing, and Bosnia and Adem tiptoed toward it.

Sitting at the table, a bowl of coffee in front of her, was Sophie, looking like a frightened little animal, so beautiful, so delicate, her eyes red and swollen, her upper lip split—she was holding a compress to it, trying awkwardly to hide the blood trickling from it—Sophie, who was so young and who had known only this war waged within the secrecy of the newlyweds' four walls by Mirsad, whom she had loved so much before he turned into a daily tormentor; Sophie, who was trying in spite of everything to smile but could not with the split lip, and who said to them, "I made you some coffee. Mirsad has gone to work. He'll be back late tonight. Please forgive us."

Forgive us! How could she say "forgive us" when she wasn't guilty? Bosnia could not abide this weakness of women, which had outraged her since she was little, at least since the age of reason. She was remembering so many scenes this morning, facing this fragile girl sitting in a miserable kitchenette in the middle of dozens of cages crammed with postmodern prisoners in these slabs of identical grey buildings blocking the horizon, where you didn't know any more which direction was which, or if the wind was the *tramontane* or if it was from the ends of the earth lashed by the icy storm, where the heavens were lost to any vision of the sublime, where human beings tore each other apart and made war on each other when it no longer existed around them, creating it from scratch. She was remembering so many scenes from when she was eight years old, or maybe ten or twelve, crossing the countryside with her father to sell vegetables, and they would go into house after house where a woman would be sitting in front of a steaming cup of coffee with a brood of scabby, fly-covered, snot-nosed kids hanging on her apron strings, and when the woman gave her father a cup of coffee and her, Sabaheta, a bowl of milk, she would say "forgive us" and try to hide a split lip or a black eye. Then Bosnia came back to Sophie, fragile and sweet and beautiful—she, too, guilty and ashamed of a misdeed that was not even hers. Bosnia vowed she would return to school as soon as she could and would become a doctor of the mind and do something about that war, the one waged against so many women in the world, even women in countries of peace and democracy, even women in countries where the most beautiful books in the world were written. She would continue to read those books that had forged her awareness and her view of the world, but this morning, facing that helpless Sophie, she was determined that she would be a doctor of the mind, a doctor of minds without borders.

The whole morning, Sophie told them of the life of torment she had known since the day after her marriage to Mirsad. She had just graduated from the *lycée* and was about to start university in geography when Mirsad came into her life and she fell totally in love, "Love at first sight, if you only knew!" Her parents, workers in Lille, had seen only her happiness. She was "the prettiest," her father had said on the day of the wedding, which took place at the Lille City Hall—her family had been agnostic Communists and "agnostic atheists for generations," her grandfather always said—and she wore white. Sophie showed them photographs of herself radiant beside Mirsad, who looked gentle as a lamb. Then they moved to Lyon, where Mirsad had a job as a labourer in a food market. In the train that took the lovebirds across France, Mirsad informed her that she would have to forget about going to university, he wanted her to be a "homemaker." She didn't worry about it, telling herself they'd see about that later, and in the meantime, she would quietly apply to university. And they smothered each other in kisses until they got to the apartment and to the bed, where they loved each other again and again until daybreak.

Her hell began that evening when Mirsad came home from work. There was one blow, then another, and then more. He forbade her to leave the apartment without permission, and he forbade her to spend even a *centime*, or to receive mail or telephone calls, or to write letters or even keep a diary, and he kept constant watch on her. Sophie wanted to run away, but how could she do it and where would she go? She did not want to call her parents. Nor her friends in Lille. She was ashamed. Her humiliation hurt as much as the beatings. She thought of suicide and often wanted to die, but every time, her love of life won out, it was so strong, although she did not know where it came from. And her love for Mirsad turned into fear, a terrible fear, as if Mirsad had become a wild animal. And the fear became hatred, an appalling hatred, as if the blood in her veins had turned to gall, and she was filled with a cold rage. She could kill him, she thought to herself during her long hours of loneliness and terror, she could kill him, but she did not have the power to do it. And this desire for his death, combined with the impotence to carry it out, made her heart and mind sterile. In the emptiness of her days, she could no longer think or read, or dream. And she hated herself. It was this hatred of herself that kept her alive.

Then two angels had arrived. "Adem and Bosnia, you came to me. Take me with you!"

The plans did not take long. By noon, Sophie's few belongings were packed. First they would go to a hotel for a night or two. "Not far from the Rhône. Not far from the water," Bosnia said. They would take a big room, with two double beds. With the money Milovan had given them, they would have enough to get by. In two hours, Sophie had become their little sister to be protected. To be saved. Adem and Bosnia were familiar with combat, they were seasoned. They knew how to counter the war-in-peacetime waged by Mirsad and his bloodthirsty ilk. They had not expected their arrival in a quiet land to be like this—but never again! They had fought there and they could fight here. As for Sophie, she would gain strength, she would learn, she was young, like them, she had a lot going for her—the combined ages of all three of them were less than seventy. Sophie thanked them and hugged them. Adem wrote a note on a scrap of paper and Bosnia added her signature, and they left it on the table.

Mirsad, we're leaving with Sophie. For good. We are warriors against all wars and against all the militias of the world, military or civilian. Don't try to find her.

I'm sorry to be the cousin of a bastard who abuses women. One day, what you have done

will be punished like any other crime against
humanity. We will fight to establish such an
international criminal tribunal.

Adem
Bosnia

Sophie wrote nothing. But beside the note, she placed the veil he had made her wear, which he would tear off in a rage before forcing himself on her.

Before closing the door of the apartment, Sophie asked, "What do you think, should I throw these keys in the garbage can downstairs?" And then, in the elevator, she said, "I forgot to tell you … this morning, he was beating me because of the way I supposedly looked at you, Adem, last night when you arrived. Does that make any sense?"

XVIII

SOME OTHERWISE ORDINARY EVENTS in a lifetime seem to concentrate time so that a day has as much impact as a week or even a year. The day they went to the refugee centre in Lyon was such a day. They had gone to a charming little hotel in the old city, from which they could see the Saône River through the little panes of the large window of their room, and smell the sweetness of its waters wafting to their beds. Later they crossed the river on the Pont de la Feuillée to go, by way of Rue d'Algérie, to the art museum and the opera, Boulevard Jean Moulin and the Rhône, on which, in the late afternoon, they saw boats shimmering like flaming swords in the October sun. Bosnia, Sophie, and Adem went to the Bosnian refugee centre, where they were greeted with warmth and friendliness, and where Adem telephoned Milovan, with whom it had been agreed that "his two children" would go live in Paris with his brother Toscan, who, like Milovan, was a jeweller, and who would be expecting them in his big apartment not far from his shop in the fifth arrondissement. Toscan had no children. After the death of his first wife, he had emigrated to France and in the fifties had married Hannah, whom Milovan had met just once, during the only trip he had ever made to Paris. "She's a remarkable woman, Hannah, you'll see, kids. You'll like her a lot," he said.

Milovan even told Adem that he would come and see them in Paris as soon as his work permitted. He wanted to take them to Toscan's notary to will them the inheritance they would need "to pay for your studies and start out on the right foot. Poor kids, who've known too many trials, Insh'Allah!" And when Bosnia took the receiver, Milovan, trying to hide his tears, said, "Little Bosnia, you can call your mama. I had a telephone put in for her. She was so happy. She's waiting for your call."

As absolute as her silence had been in the war, her words now seemed inexhaustible. Bosnia let her mother cull little anecdotes from everyday events without interrupting, until the flow subsided on its own and the cheerful voice running along the magic thread between the two countries suddenly asked, "And you, little Sabaheta, how are you doing?" But Bosnia barely had time to say anything about herself before her mother started up again with endless disjointed stories about her life there that came one after the other in parentheses within parentheses. Bosnia listened to some of the more familiar ones and let the others float off into thin air. It did not bore her to listen to her mother chatter on like this. It reminded her vaguely of when she was very little, when she would press her ear to that soft warm body and be enveloped and soothed by the flow of her mother's words, the meaning of which mostly escaped her. This voice of today took her back to those times of sweetness when death and sorrow had not yet knocked at their door.

Bosnia spoke to her of her happiness in her new life, told her what she had been doing, and asked her again if she wanted them to come and take her back to live with them. But Mamouni, hiding the tears that were welling up, answered in a voice that was suddenly serious, "No. I would rather love you in absence than uproot myself." She again told her story of the old oak tree that mustn't be uprooted, and she declared that to expatriate her body from the soil where the body of her beloved Ismet lay would be to uproot her spirit and deport her soul, and that, even if she were with her cherished daughter, she would again begin to wander in the dark, icy corridors she had known among the mad. No, she wanted to stay in Sarajevo—"But you, you'll come next summer, you'll come with Adem. I'll let you have my bedroom, I'll sleep on the sofa in the dining room. You know, I get along very well with my landlady, Liliana, we talk a lot, we do our shopping together, and our cooking too, and in the evening, we play cards with our neighbours—they're all women, there are almost no men left in the city, many have died, many more are still in prison. There's that good Milovan, who comes to see us from time to time, he says you're his children. We still have no news of Mumo."

Bosnia was still on the phone with her mother when she heard earsplitting cries of joy coming from the foyer of the centre. She just had time to say goodbye before she saw Adem throw himself into the arms of a vibrant, ecstatic young man. It was obviously a major reunion— which would soon be confirmed by the introductions. The young man was Stefan, Adem's best friend from before the war, when they were both studying law at the University of Sarajevo. Stefan the Croat, but people then didn't make distinctions between Muslims, Serbs, and Croats—they were all Bosnians, even Yugoslavs. The masters of war had not yet set them against each other with hate propaganda and racist talk. Stefan, like many, had disappeared during the siege of Sarajevo, but here he was now, here in the flesh, in this centre in Lyon where he had, in fact, just dropped by to check his mail. Stefan had returned to his law studies in Paris, and was working as an interpreter at UNESCO, thanks to a friend, Thibault, who had a job there. He was supposed to leave again for Paris the next day. The two boys hugged, and then held each other by the shoulders and looked at each other again, laughing, almost crying, because they were neither dead nor maimed. Both of them had known the horror, as they would later recount to each other, but today their paths had brought them back together very much alive, they could hardly believe it. Amid all the excitement, Adem introduced his friend to Bosnia and Sophie, who had been watching the scene with tenderness and wonder, as if they were witnessing a birth or some other event that by its nature is able to ward off the spell of death.

The four of them went to a neighbourhood bistro. They were hungry and they were thirsty. The two boys talked and talked, they had so much to tell each other—

would life be long enough to fill the gulf of absence between them, the trench that the war had dug in their friendship?—they talked mostly about the future while they ate and drank, keeping silent on the tragedy each suspected the other had experienced, their glasses clinking with every plan they made. It was agreed that they would all go to Paris in the little used car Stefan had bought with his savings, which was old but ran well. "It's something I'd always dreamed of," he told the happy gathering. Bosnia, her heart in the celebration but her eyes fixed on the window and the river running south, was drifting along the water towards the delta of the Rhône and on to Marseille, where she would swim before going up towards the Lubéron and to Manosque, where "the gods and the grasses lived their slow eternal life." She said, "Listen, boys," and quoted them those beautiful words of Giono, from *Naissance de l'Odyssée*. In a sweet state of euphoria, she asked if they wanted to go to the Mediterranean and then to Mont d'Or, before heading for Paris. The boys answered, "We'll see. Let's sleep on it." But Bosnia had no doubt the four of them would take that trip she had so often imagined. Then she suddenly became aware that Sophie was drifting away, no longer seeing them, lost in a bottomless well of sadness. She was shivering amid the warmth of her friends' reunion and their plans; she was cold and miserable, as if there were within her a vast, unnameable desert of ice, and Bosnia put her arms around her.

The four friends left the bistro at closing time. Arm in arm, they set out through the streets of Lyon, crossing the Saône again and heading back to the little hotel, with Stefan accompanying them. He would pick them up in the morning. Between two songs from the Yugoslavia of their childhood, he had told Bosnia, "It's a good idea to go south first. I would like to know your Giono's country. Besides, I haven't taken a vacation in a long time. That's so beautiful—'the gods and the grasses lived their slow eternal life.' It must be magnificent there. And I miss the sea."

When they were in bed in their big room with the paned windows that let the sweet smell of water enter to wash over them in their beds, Bosnia and Adem could hear Sophie crying quietly, mixing with that sweet water her salty streams so long held back. After all, she had only just left her brute of a husband that morning, and, as Bosnia whispered very, very softly in Adem's ear, in order to wash herself clean of that dirty war, she might need to bathe in tears for as many days and nights as she had endured with him. Then the sound of her regular breathing told them she had finally fallen asleep. Kissing Adem, Bosnia whispered, "Do you think she'll know happiness one day?"

XIX

THE LANDSCAPE STREAMED BY in the cobalt morning, as if the sea had flowed into the sky, painting streaks of zaffre on the autumn ochres. They had earlier passed close to the grey profile of Mont Ventoux and, just after Avignon, had seen in the distance the jagged gate of the Alpilles, which they had only to open to enter the garden they were approaching. Sophie was sleeping in the back beside Bosnia, who was daydreaming, and Adem and Stefan were in the front, speaking from time to time—they had so much to tell each other, and there were so few people who could understand what they had been through in the war—and the girls in the back did not disturb them. They were their "third ear," their loving sisters, and they understood everything, even Sophie, who was marked by the nightmare from which she had just awakened. Bosnia knew that soon the jagged gate of the Alpilles would open to the garden of water she had been waiting so long to see, the Mediterranean. In her head she wrote a note to Adem, because the day before, an evil shadow had been cast on their young love so tender and so gentle. The four of them had gone to the Bosnian refugee centre for a little celebration after a speech by a Paris intellectual, an expert on war. They had listened to that elegant, charming man, who was an artist with words, making every idea he presented sound completely fresh. Bosnia, enthralled, had gone to talk to the handsome philosopher during the party, a glass of champagne in her hand, and had inadvertently found herself in his arms, dancing and telling her story of the war, which he wanted to hear in detail and even asked to record—and to "pay for this work"—and suddenly, in the arms of this magnificent talker, Bosnia had no longer felt the floor beneath her feet, she had felt dizzy and had gone to sit down. At the very moment she was saying to him, "I'm not fodder for your pen," she saw a storm cloud of jealousy pass over Adem's dark gaze, a jealousy she had until then only imagined through books, and in a flash, she was with him and had led him outside where the air was pure and cool, but the harm had already been done, and despite her attempts to explain, Adem wouldn't say anything. He must have gone back to his dear ones dead and murdered, he was very far from her, absorbed by his reopened wounds, and in her mind this cobalt morning on the way to those waters that could wash and heal, she wrote, "Love, my love, is stronger than evil and stronger than war, you'll see; love, my love, is what I will give you to the end of our days."

Bosnia tried to find other words but there were no more. "Why do death and pain have more words than love?" she wondered, closing her eyes and beginning to doze. "Why am I, who wanted to see everything in this mythic Provence, giving it up already?" And she fell asleep. In her dream was the handsome Paris philosopher who had wooed her by chatting about the war, and then her belly really hurt, a cramp tore through her bowels, and a stream of blood gushed to the ground, carrying a purple egg of miscarriage that the philosopher was about to open with little surgical scissors, and in the distance, she could see Adem, Adila, and Marina trying to run to her but sinking into the clay, and Bosnia shouted "Mama, Mamouni!" but no one heard her. And then there was a warm hand on her cheek wiping away her tears and another hand holding hers, and Adem was waking her slowly, covering her fingers with little kisses, Adem smiling at her and saying, "You know, my friends, when life has taken you into hell, sometimes in dreams, you return to the world of the damned. And then, you come back as if nothing has happened, and you love," just as the car was turning off to the right onto a little road to the sea, which they could see now. Adem smiled at Bosnia, who dried her tears and revived. She looked at him. Then she saw the sea. That sea whose very name held a land of promise in it: the Mediterranean!

To describe the blue of the sky melting into the blue of the sea, to describe this eternity of sky and water with no horizon line, to find a single word that existed in no one language but that would bring them all together to bear witness to this perfection and then contemplate it in silence till the end of time, to respond to this beauty with silence, a silence broken only by the beat of the surf and the cries of the birds. So thought Bosnia while she sat on the sand with her companions, all of them silently gazing into the distance, slowly sifting the sun-warmed sand with their hands, their feet already bare—shoes and socks strewn on the beach—bodies leaning against the rocky wall of an inlet where they had spontaneously taken refuge, alone, sheltered from intruders, alone and together in the majesty of the day. The little local road had taken them there, somewhere outside Marseille, and they felt as if they were at the end of the earth without a soul around, in a corner of the world, finally, that seemed to have been waiting for them, to give them all its space and all its time. A light breeze from the hills, which must have been the tail end of the mistral, carried to the salt and iodine of the sea the smells of the little valleys stretching below the mountain, of the farms dotting the limestone relief, the scrubland intermingled with ploughed fields, the dry grasses full of spicy fragrance, the clay cracking under the sun's hot rays, the carefully tended gardens and orchards, alluvial deposits of the ages, a composite country carried to their nostrils by that gentle wind.

Bosnia stretched out on the sand, breathing, inhaling the smells. Pressing her ear to the ground to better hear the music of the surf, she wanted to become one with the vibrato of the sea. She welcomed all those smells come down from the mountain with the last notes of the mistral, she gave thanks to the wind, to all the winds of the earth, to this breath without borders that travels all the countries and all the seas, she thanked it very softly and named it patron saint of all the migrants of the world. Adem was

135

strctchcd out beside her, and she took his warm hand and lay down full length on his body, and soon they were naked, like their two friends already frolicking like children in the water, and soon they in turn dove into the waves, with foam splashing and laughter and kisses, and soon they had run further down the beach and were making love, the juices of mouths and sexes mingled, and Adem's tears too. Adem, lying in Bosnia's arms, had found total release, and the shadows of his dead had suddenly vanished. He spoke into Bosnia's ear, as if he had finally left the edge of the precipice in the ruins: "Little sister, I will always love you, until the end of my days." Bosnia thought again of the Hiroshima of Sarajevo, of her dead friends Adila and Marina, and then of her father. "I love you too," she said to Adem, adding, "do you think we will be able to go back to Bosnia-Herzegovina next summer and bury them all?"

When Sophie and Stefan came back from their swim, they found Adem and Bosnia asleep.

"So, are the lovebirds going to come and eat?"

Stefan's voice brought Adem back from far away. With Bosnia's head resting in the hollow of his shoulder, he saw the picnic laid out on the tablecloth on the beach, and Sophie and Stefan chatting, glasses in hand. When the cork on the bottle of rosé had popped, he had heard the sound of a gunshot and found himself in the Black Forest hunting with his uncle, and then eating roast venison with the family, his grandmother crying—but they did not know why—his father cradling his sister, who was very little, and his mother serving and laughing heartily. Adem said to Bosnia, "This is the first time since the war that I've dreamed, you know," and then, "I'm hungry, little sister. What about you?"

XX

THE FOUR OF THEM sat in silence on the summit of Mont
d'Or, contemplating the valley of the Durance as far as
the Lubéron hills, which they had crossed the day
before, delighted. Their gaze drifted to the vaulted sky
in the northeast, where they could make out the Alps,
and to the other sky to the south, an expanse extending
so far that they could easily imagine the sea below. They
sat in silence accompanied only by the mistral, whose
choruses they listened to without speaking. Bosnia,
her body still warm from the pleasure of love, heard in
the wind's breath something like a lament from her
dead friends Adila and Marina, and saw them again,
hand in hand, laid out in that garden of stones in
Sarajevo, torn from the immensity of life by a simple
little thing, the explosion of a shell, and Bosnia held
within her body still warm from love, resonating with
lament and pain, a soft melody like a counterpoint to
the music of the gusting wind.

Bosnia, Sophie, Adem, and Stefan had climbed on
foot from Manosque, where they had left the car

parked "on Giono's street," as Bosnia had insisted—and no one had objected. After all, it was in a way for her that they had made this trip. Adem had even confided to Stefan that he had this crazy desire to give her amazing gifts, he really didn't know why, he had never felt this way before. They had climbed for a good hour and a half, knapsacks on their backs with sandwiches and bottles of water, joking and teasing each other along the way, stopping to admire a flower or a shrub or a stone. They were happy and sang songs from their childhood. Sophie, her voice a flute-like soprano, had taught them "Le temps des cerises" and "Nini-peau-d'chien." Then, crying "À la Bastille," they reached the summit, and suddenly, in the turbulence of the wind that came from all four directions, the four of them bowed their bodies in unison and sat down in silence, each on his or her rock or clump of earth, gazing at the variegated horizon, each deep in his or her own thoughts, immersed in the unfathomable solitude that mountains, wherever they are, always evoke.

Bosnia took out the book the handsome Paris philosopher had left for her at the hotel, with a little note. She had found it at the reception desk the day after they met and hadn't mentioned it to Adem, not wanting to hurt him for nothing. She found the book itself beautiful, as well as its title. It was *Conversation in the Mountains*, by Paul Celan, a poet she did not know. Still fixed on the vision of her dead friends, she opened it at random, as she always did at first with a book, and she had only to read one passage to know she would love this book: "I on my way to myself, up here."* She closed it again and held it in her hands like a talisman, and right then she understood that her need to climb Mont d'Or, which she had associated since her first reading of Giono with her desire to know this writer better, was in fact a need to encounter her own inner self, Sabaheta-Bosnia. She repeated the phrase to herself, "I on my way to myself, up here," and understood that deep within her, regardless of her immeasurable love for Adem and for the children she hoped for with him, there would still always be a refuge, warm and inaccessible to others, an infinite solitude—as if the abyss and the summit had been conceived to illuminate each other, as the breath of the earth revealed to her through the wind—she knew it immediately, and she would know it until the end of her days. She said in a throaty voice, as if she had come back from a dangerous expedition, "I on my way to myself, up here." No one said a word, no one asked for an explanation, the phrase floated with the music of the air, as they yielded to that moment of solemnity.

The beauty outside could not mask the anxiety all four of them were feeling that day. For Adem and Bosnia, who had discussed it the evening before, the trip back to Paris the next day, while exciting, was also a little scary. What would he be like, this Toscan whose home they were going to? How would they cope with the problems and difficulties of sorting out their refugee status? Where and how could they register for graduate

---

* Translated by John Felstiner.

studies—and in Bosnia's case, what to study? Of course, Stefan and the NGOs there would help them, but the unknown was still scary. Bosnia had said, "I would rather face a known enemy with weapons in my hands in the guerrillas than take on Paris, that mythical Hydra with its thousands of shining heads." During the war, they had dreamed of that city of learning, peace, and freedom, and now, the day before they were finally to encounter it, it seemed threatening, and they both felt in their bones the double strangeness they had whispered to each other in the howling wind: the strangeness of coming from elsewhere and being strangers to the city, but also the strangeness of possibly not recognizing this city they had so long dreamed of. They also had a paradoxical feeling that they were old and battle-scarred despite their youth, as if being dispossessed immigrants in a country living in a state of peace and well-being had altered their ages.

As for Sophie, she seemed to have become mute, and Stefan wasn't doing much better. Eating their sandwiches, they were huddling together shoulder to shoulder, like two kittens in a ray of sunshine, their eyes gazing off into the distance, their hair blowing in the wind. The two got along like brother and sister, and Sophie, an only child, was overjoyed at finding this sensitive, thoughtful, affectionate young man who, unlike all the others, did not want to get her into bed as soon as he set eyes on her. She didn't really know why there was this fraternal feeling between them. Since adolescence, she had known nothing but flirting, silence, scheming, and conflict with boys, and never this closeness made up of trust and confidences. Her anxiety today was related to the strange thing that was happening in her body—her belly was warm, she wasn't getting her period, her breasts were swollen and sensitive, and she sometimes felt a little nauseous. She was obviously pregnant, but barely dared admit it to herself. The idea of bringing into the world the child of that brute Mirsad seemed like her worst nightmare—"I must be dreaming," she thought, "I'm going to wake up"—but at the same time, she felt that stirring of the heart, that call of life rising from her belly—"A human being will live within me, it's not possible"—and she too felt doubly a stranger: in the most private place within her was a creature that was still absolutely unknown, that perturbed her whole body, that came from a man who had abused and raped her, a man she had left because she hated him and yet who survived in her belly like a barbarian who had branded her on the inside. "What can I do?" wondered Sophie. "What can I tell my parents?"—she hadn't yet told them of her escape— "Who can I talk to?" Never had she felt so alone, and the fact that her aloneness was now shared by the intruder in her belly made it even more intolerable. It all seemed like an impassable desert. "Talking to my three new friends may be the only possible oasis," she thought, but the words did not come; there were none that really expressed the inhabited emptiness she had been living in for the past few days.

That evening in a restaurant, around an excellent ratatouille and a good bottle of wine, they were finally able to talk about the things that were bothering them. Stefan opened the floodgates by announcing point blank what he had never told even his good friend

Adem: he was gay, homosexual, and wanted to say both words to make it clearly understood. He had always desired guys, ever since desire had come into his life at the age of twelve, when he had fallen in love with his teacher but couldn't talk to anyone about it. Later, he had had plenty of affairs, always guilty and secret, until he fell in love for real at the beginning of the war in Croatia. He had lost his lover in an artillery barrage— he'd found him under the debris, his body cut in two— since then, his own body was cut in two, one part remaining in the Dubrovnik cemetery and the other being dragged first to Sarajevo, where he went to study, and then to the refugee centre in Lyon, and finally, to Paris. "I'm not even searching for love any more, there is a death within me that has destroyed all desire. It's a strange feeling, as if the mutilation of my lover's body had amputated all love from me," said Stefan. He continued telling his story for a long time and said how relieved he was to tell them all this and how happy it made him sometimes when he went walking in the gay neighbourhood of Paris, in the Marais, to see young men walking around and showing their love freely, and some nights, he would go into the bars to watch them laugh and enjoy themselves, they who must, like him, have suffered so much and for so many years, having to endure the radical strangeness of their condemned loves. Then he felt a sense of solidarity with their past shame and their present joy.

"In my Catholic Croatia, homosexuality is either a sin or an illness or a crime. In your Bosnia-Herzegovina, it's not much better, your imams are as hypocritical as our priests. If I have left religion, all religions, it's because of that hypocrisy. And if I have no more faith, it's because I can't tolerate the idea of a God who would powerlessly witness all the evil and all the atrocities we have known, a God who could have seen my lover with his body sliced in two without coming to put him together again, a God I was taught was omnipotent, a God who could have seen all that, who sees all if He is God, without taking me in his arms and putting my lover together and giving him back to me. My faith is rooted in this world, in my humanitarian work with Avocats sans Frontières. I may not be able to create a paradise on earth—so much of it is rotten— but I'm going to at least try to make sure all the bastards who do the work of death get convicted and give the victims back a little of the dignity they've taken from them."

Sophie understood why Stefan was like a brother to her. "The world should be full of such unthreatening men," she thought, stroking her warm, fragile belly, and decided not to divulge her own tragedy that evening. She took Stefan's hand, covered it with kisses, and pressed her body even closer to his. It was so reassuring to love a man who loved you for something other than sex!

They drank until late at night. They had gone from the restaurant to the big room the four of them were occupying. They drank themselves delirious, until the words took them to places where they could weep with laughter and laugh with weeping.

Before falling asleep, Adem asked, "Tomorrow, should we take the road through the Alps?"

XXI

ON THE TELEPHONE, Toscan had told them to come directly to the apartment if they arrived after the shop closed at seven. "We'll be expecting you. Drive carefully, kids," he had added. The jeweller's shop and the apartment were both in the fifth arrondissement, not far from each other, the shop on Port-Royal and the apartment on Rue du Fer à Moulin. They entered Paris through the Porte d'Italie, and decided to take a look at the store, just a peek in the front window. Then, all four feeling a bit nervous, they turned onto Avenue des Gobelins and then on to the charming little Rue du Fer à Moulin, where they parked the car beside a tiny park lined with plane trees, very close to the building where Hannah and Toscan were waiting for them. They took Bosnia's and Adem's baggage out of the car. There wasn't really a lot; just two bags each and not very big ones, but all the same, they felt uncomfortable. Even though Milovan had no end of good things to say about his brother Toscan, they were still imposing on a perfect stranger with all their things. "I want to go home," Bosnia whispered in Adem's ear. "Me too," Adem replied, as the four turned to look at the moon above the branches. It was full, bright, and beautiful, reassuring them with its velvety roundness, and Bosnia, regaining her courage, pressed the four numbers of the entry code that opened the heavy wooden door of the porte-cochère to give them a glimpse of an imposing entrance and then a garden that was obviously well cared for and lush and, even in winter, was still fragrant. They were all breathing in the goodness of the sleeping plants when suddenly they saw snowflakes gently falling in the young moonlit night, laying a white path to Stairwell C. They turned on the light, delighted with this welcome from the elements, and started climbing the stairs to the third floor in single file.

(On the road not far from Grenoble, where Bosnia had wanted to stop because of her fondness for Stendhal, they had discussed Sophie's fate at great length. She hardly thought about Mirsad any more, as if that nightmare had vanished as fast as it had come, but she was going to have to return to Lille to face her parents, to explain to them and tell them about the divorce proceedings, which Stefan would help her with—but she would not tell them she was pregnant, since, in any case, she had decided to have an abortion. Before and after Grenoble, they had talked for hours and listened to Sophie's confidences, her tears, her laughter, her whispers, and her declarations, because she was both fragile and strong, this young woman who had mistaken torture and possession for love, but who, in an act of astonishing power, had snapped the chain that bound her to her tormentor. Together, they had calculated, analyzed, and considered, and finally, Sophie had decided to speak frankly to her parents—after the abortion, which she would not mention—and to come and live in Paris, where Stefan was offering to share an apartment with her, and, above all—something she was experiencing as an incredible victory—not to go to university in geography, but to choose to become what, deep in her heart, she had always wanted to be, a painter, an artist. On the road from Grenoble to Paris, Sophie had repeated it, "I'm going to enroll at the Beaux-Arts!" And on the strength of that certainty, with the prospect of finally fulfilling her wish, she knew that her parents, who had the means, would help her.)

When they spoke to him on the telephone, Toscan had warmly invited Bosnia and Adem's friends to dinner that evening. "My children's friends are my children," he had said. They couldn't get over being treated like this by an absolute stranger, and they entered the country of peace with the same amazement, the same blind lack of awareness, as when they plunged into territories mined with the hatred of war. And Toscan had added, "Hannah will be delighted to take you in, you'll stay at our place as long as you need to, we're expecting you."

It was with this uncertainty, some anxiety, and the thoughts and fatigue of the journey, but also their appreciation of the beauty of Rue du Fer à Moulin and the fragrant, snowy garden, that they reached the third floor. They looked at each other, half laughing, half apprehensive, and stopped to catch their breath. Bosnia nodded to Adem, who pressed the doorbell with his index finger.

The door opened to reveal a friendly face with a wide smile. It was Toscan, who looked like his brother Milovan, only a little older—"Like a twin," he always said with his hearty laugh. They were greeted by the mingled aromas from the kitchen and from bouquets of flowers placed throughout the apartment, roses, violets, and pansies, the extension of the winter garden in the courtyard below. From the kitchen came a frail-looking woman who appeared even older than her companion— as Bosnia remarked the next day to the other three, "She couldn't be much less than eighty"—with a very pale, wrinkled face that, despite the suffering one might suspect in her past, seemed to radiate a tenderness and a joy whose origin was not even imaginable. "I'm Toscan, and this is Hannah" was followed by a long session of hugs, as if they were all long-lost friends who had missed each other terribly. "And yet, only two minutes before, we hadn't known each other," they all thought, but friendship has a way of erasing time, playing tricks with clocks, hourglasses, and calendars.

"There are miracles in peacetime as in wartime," said Bosnia. "For people who didn't know each other, we certainly missed each other a lot." They all seemed to agree, as no one asked for an explanation.

"Come in, children," invited Hannah and Toscan. And then they filed through the central rooms of the huge apartment, living room and dining room in one, separated by a shiny black baby grand piano, open, with sheet music neatly arranged—"Hannah is the musician," said Toscan—with furniture of warm wood with a lovely patina, Middle Eastern carpets, vases, beautiful paintings, and in the dining area, a gleaming silver candelabra set on an embroidered unbleached linen tablecloth, with six place settings in silver and old china, and elegant cut glass goblets for the wine, which was "from my wine merchant," as Toscan said, "a great wine at a reasonable price." But when they tasted it, the young people knew that a reasonable price for Toscan would have meant a big expense for them. None of them had ever seen such a luxurious home and yet they felt completely at ease, their hosts were so modest, charming, and unpretentious.

While Hannah made the final preparations for dinner, Toscan took Bosnia and Adem upstairs "to show you your rooms and let you freshen up." In the former garret that had been converted into guests' quarters, they found a pretty room under the eaves, with dormer windows, a "library"—a large study with a table and armchairs—and an ultra-modern bathroom. Bosnia and Adem put down their bags. Bosnia clasped Toscan's hands, tears in her eyes, and said, "It's too much, Monsieur Toscan, it's much too much for us." And Toscan stroked her hair, a little flustered, a little awkward in expressing his affection, and unaccustomed to being with young people, and said, "No, no, my dear, after what you've been through, you know, Milovan told me about you two, this could never be too much, life can never pamper you enough in the future." Then he turned away, as if he had said too much.

(After getting up the next day, Bosnia and Adem contemplated the view over the roofs of Paris. They were greeted by a clear sky on that first morning, and their amazed eyes were drawn to the dome of the Panthéon and, on the other side, to the tops of the trees in the Jardin des Plantes, which looked like Chinese brushes that had been dipped into the translucent waters of the Seine a little further away.)

Despite their fatigue, the four travellers drank to their arrival in Paris in a state of euphoria. They were impressed by the slow ritual they witnessed as their elders officiated over the seemingly sacred ceremony of tasting—smelling the bouquet, wetting their lips, and then rolling the wine around in their mouths for a long time—with a delicious Sancerre from the mysterious wine merchant who had "great wines at reasonable prices" that they would discover one day.

"You'll rest up here," said Hannah, "before you start making arrangements for studies and work. Tonight, try not to think too much, just enjoy yourselves. You know, you shouldn't feel obligated to talk about your war, or uncomfortable about talking about it as much as you like. I come from a war too. I was born in Hungary, and basically, I was born into war. I'm Jewish. A survivor of the Shoah, of Auschwitz, where all the members of my two families were killed. Some people don't want to talk about it, and that's their right. Others don't want to hear about it any more. I tell non-Jews who don't want to hear about it any more that as far as I'm concerned, I'll keep telling the story for as many years as there were Jews murdered, which means I'll be talking for the next six million years. And even after I die, if I still have a mouth in the next life, I'll keep on talking about it for eternity."

Strangely, Hannah's talk about death and genocide made Bosnia, Adem, Sophie, and Stefan feel better, as if she had gone right to the thing that was causing them so much pain, the thing they often felt like talking about—but who would want to listen, who in a peaceful country would want to hear such horror, who would have the strength to endure the stories written in the ink of still-open wounds?

Paradoxically, when they sat down and Hannah served her lamb with flageolets and green beans, and Toscan served the decanted Bordeaux, and the clamour of talk and laughter started up again, they could have devoured the food plates and all, they were so hungry and the aromas so mouth-watering.

Toscan asked everyone, "Who wants to taste this wine for me?"

XXII

SITTING UP IN HER BED in total darkness with Adem sleeping peacefully beside her, Bosnia felt for her flashlight. She'd had enough of this feeling that she was sleeping between two worlds, and she wanted to go to the nice armchair in the library and wrap herself from shoulders to feet in a warm shawl, she wanted to get things straight in her head and to read—there were so many books she would love here. Yes, to read, or just to dream, but waking dreams, not the illogical, anxiety-producing ones in which she had been mired since her first sleep of this long night when she kept waking up and falling back into the inextricable tangles of horrendous stories, balanced precariously on half of a concrete bridge that had broken in two in the middle of the ocean, over a void, an abyss, with roaring waves sucking her in, or other times, a moment, an infinite moment, later, in a strange house that became a labyrinth, with a door that opened onto nothing or a stairway leading nowhere, with someone chasing her, and then suddenly a threatening Mumo, with a long beard and a dagger pointed at her, was trying to tear her from Adem's arms, cover her with a veil, and take her back to Bosnia. And then she had screamed, which had finally transported her out of the infernal dream, and she had sat straight up in bed, groping for the little flashlight she couldn't find.

She tried to understand where her torment was coming from—it was so much the opposite of her present happiness. Hadn't she fallen asleep curled up against Adem, who was elated by recent events? He had covered her with a thousand little kisses and joyfully whispered sweet nothings, they loved each other so much, and then she had let herself sink into a bed softer than any she had ever known; she had smelled the fragrance of lavender on the sheets and pillowcases of soft linen and gone over in her mind the animated conversation of the evening. She had thought about Hannah's indefatigable good humour even when remembering the concentration camps, and her tragicomic spirit that was like a second skin of the soul and that unassumingly created a distance between her and the world. Hannah's laughter was neither mocking nor sarcastic. It was like a sidelong glance at things. Bosnia tried in the darkness to characterize it, to find the words to describe this laughter that could be weeping, this laughter that, out of courtesy to the guests Hannah loved to entertain, stopped short of cynicism. And then Bosnia had followed the thread back to Hannah's story of what she called her "atheist enlightenment"—they had laughed till they cried at that story of "deconversion," even Toscan, who knew it by heart, and who had also "deconverted," in his case from Islam, "ages ago."

But Hannah had had an "atypical life, you understand, children." Her Jewish Hungarian family was made up of Communists on her father's side and rabbis on her mother's side, but her mother herself had "deconverted" in marrying her father, and had become "horror of horrors, a believer in Communism." But in Auschwitz—"History sometimes takes surprising turns"—Hannah had met Western European Communists from the Catholic tradition, and one day one of them had given her two books by Paul Claudel, which she liked so much she wanted to read everything by that poet. Years later—after her liberation from Auschwitz in 1945, and then her deportation to a Soviet camp in Siberia, and after going to Israel, where she lived for five years on a kibbutz, where she did not like the communitarianism and proselytizing—when she had arrived in France, with which she had "fallen in love at first sight, a love that has never died," she wanted to reread Claudel. She bought all his books, and she went to Notre-Dame and touched the column in front of the altar to the Virgin, where he had had his conversion at the end of the nineteenth century, comparing himself to Paul of Tarsus on the road to Damascus, and she in turn converted, following that impulse. She made an appointment with the priest at the cathedral, who was astonished by her decision, which he said was "unusual in this postmodern, deconstructionist era," and who agreed to hear her confession, give her communion, and direct her to catechism classes.

But one day, when she looked at all the madness and stupidity of the murderous twentieth century, all the genocidal conflicts in the world, and saw that peoples were still being murdered on nearly every continent, and when she realized how much the entire world had declined because its stewards were squandering its riches shamelessly, one day, high in the Alps, those mountains that touched the sky, where the monks of old had built the magnificent monasteries from which they had sent forth their prayers, incantations, invocations, and petitions, century after century, to that sovereign God so that He would silence the furies down here, when she understood that the long conversations on these peaks had only been monologues at the edge of the abyss, she suddenly had her "atheist enlightenment," and she no longer believed either in earthly religions or heavenly promises. Since then, Hannah had stated, "I live free of fetters and illusions. I am free, children, do you understand?"

Sitting in the darkness of the unfamiliar bedroom, very close to Adem, whose breathing she heard, and who was her love "till the end of our days," as she often told him, Bosnia thought about the evening. Around the table, they had talked for a long time to the sound of popping corks and clinking glasses. They had held forth on the existence of God—only Sophie said she "still had faith," and the others all said, "That's your right, it doesn't hurt anybody." And Toscan had recounted something he had heard a character in a film say, a film he had recently seen on television but whose title and director he had forgotten: "God exists for those who believe in Him, and does not exist for those who don't." The evening had ended with them singing songs from the former Yugoslavia, since four of them at the table knew them well, with Hannah accompanying on the piano and Sophie dancing with Bosnia and crying hot tears on her shoulder—but no one, including Sophie herself, knew why.

No, it could not have been that wonderful evening that had propelled Bosnia into the labyrinth of a dark underworld. It must be the profusion of gloomy stories that had been accumulating inside her for so long; she could accept that, but name-of-no-God, she hated enigmas even though she found them enticing, after all she had spent a good part of her life with her nose in books, her mind bound up with the most mysterious fictions of human history, having at a very young age drunk in the *Iliad* and the *Odyssey*, Virgil's *Aeneid*, and even the *Epic of Gilgamesh*, while her high school classmates found those mandatory readings crushingly boring.

Suddenly, alone in the night, though comforted by the peaceful breathing of her love, she remembered the phone call she had made to her mother the day before yesterday, from Grenoble. But why had she mislaid that call in some inaccessible corner of her memory? "No doubt for the same reasons that make me forget when I'm in pain," she knew that much. And now, recalling her Mamouni's flat voice, a toneless voice that she no longer recognized, a voice saying, "Your brother Mumo has come back," the shock returned. No longer the same, no longer Mumo—that is what Bosnia understood from her mother's words. Her mother did not seem to be free to speak. "I'll write you, dear, I'll write you," she had said. "Mumo doesn't want to talk to you on the telephone, he wants to see you here, he wants to see you veiled." And Bosnia had finally understood that after being tortured and mutilated in the Serb prison and finally escaping, Mumo, unable to find his family, crazy with anger and despair, had one day seen the light of Allah, who had come out of the desert of his heart to lead him to the Holy Land of Saudi Arabia, from which he had just returned. Her brother had come back, that is what Bosnia had lost.

Sitting straight up in her bed in the glimmer of the dawn that was already breaking, Bosnia felt very cold. She curled up against Adem's warm body and, as she fell asleep, said, "I have something to tell you tomorrow."

XXIII

BOSNIA AWOKE TO THE SMELL of coffee and, outside, the cooing of a turtledove. The end of the night had been dreamless, as gentle and smooth as the surrounding air. On the bedside table, she saw a note from Adem. As agreed, he had left early for the day, first to meet Stefan at the bistro and then to see about what he had to do to register in law at the university and to receive credit for the two years he had done at the University of Sarajevo. After his words of love, Adem had added a little poem:

> *Between attic and basement*
> *I found this little box*
> *Splinters, holes in memory*
> *Through which the shell flows*
> *Awash in the blood of words*
> *Black sea red sea*
> *As far as love*

Bosnia kissed the paper and placed it as a bookmark in a book she had found in the library and had started reading and liked—*The Book of Promethea*, by Hélène

Cixous, which she hadn't heard of before. She opened the window wide. There was a fine curtain of rain falling on the dark brown tiles and grey stones of the house opposite, and she could see roofs far into the distance, with smoke curling up into the chilly November sky. Then the image of Mumo, bearded and mean, and the apprehensive, or possibly terrified, voice of her Mamouni came and destroyed the peaceful atmosphere. She felt cold, closed the window, dressed quickly, and went downstairs towards the smell of coffee. She was hungry, and she wanted to talk to someone. Oh, if only Hannah was there!

And Hannah was there. In the huge kitchen looking out on an inner courtyard crammed with plants and trees and with a climbing vine that, even in November, gave the impression you were in the middle of a hanging garden, one in which warm reds had pushed aside almost all the green. Hannah was there, at the end of a long rustic pine table, her head in a book, a bowl of steaming coffee at her right hand, wearing a grey dress that was from another age but incredibly becoming. She was there, beautiful in her years, wearing an old pink cardigan that gave her face a soft brightness, with her fine skin so white, whose wrinkles seemed to catch the moods of the world since time immemorial. She who had lived through the unspeakable in the Shoah, and who was still experiencing the tragedies of that time, was completely absorbed in her reading and her steaming coffee, and seemed to delight, like the child she was, in listening to the quivering of the leaves in the garden under the rain.

Hannah looked up from her book, put her index finger on the page to keep her place, and smiled at Bosnia, who, her hair dishevelled and her gaze still far away in her reveries, looked this morning like a wild child coming out of the perilous forest, bewildered by the comfort of thatched cottages. "Make yourself at home, dear. Help yourself to fruit and bread, there's butter over there, and jams and honey and Nutella, if you like. I'll just finish my paragraph, and then I'll make us some more coffee. You slept well, I hope," Hannah said, and returned to her reading. Bosnia saw the title and the author, another one she didn't know— "But I have time," she said to herself, "I'm young"—it was *L'Imprescriptible*, by Vladimir Jankélévitch. There were so many things she would like to talk about this morning with Hannah—her father's death, Mamouni's madness, the deaths of her dear Adila and Marina, her rape at the age of fourteen, the meanness of the world but also its goodness sometimes, and she thought of her love for Adem, and Milovan, their beloved protector and second father, and now the two of them, Hannah and Toscan, who had come along with such generosity at a time when their lives seemed shrouded in desperation.

She would like to talk about Mumo, about the love she had always felt for the brother she called her twin, about the false mourning she had been in all those years when she didn't know if he was dead or alive, or how and where he had died, or how and where he was living, her anguish so great that it had marked all her thoughts, all her actions, and the fighting in the guerrillas with her father, the death and burial of that father-mother Al-Lat with his teardrop of flesh, and her wild rabbit, and the lives and the deaths of her best friends ever, and even Mamouni's madness, because when she had cradled her then-mute mother in her arms in the psychiatric hospital and sung lullabies to her, Mumo disappeared-we-don't-know-where-or-how was always between them. She would like to recount her nightmares of the night before, to confide that she did not want to go back to school now, to say that one day she wanted to be a doctor of the body and the mind but that in the meantime, she just wanted to take time to rest, read, discover Paris, see museums and art galleries, go to films and concerts, walk in the parks, walk every day, and dream, and maybe even paint in her bedroom upstairs or make a studio corner in the library, the light was so beautiful up there, even in the rain, even in the half-light of dawn. She would like to say that she would have to return for a while to Sarajevo, to see her mother, whom she worried about, and to face Mumo, a prospect that terrified her, because, as brave as she had been in battle against enemies, she felt helpless and afraid in front of her big twin brother.

She would have to look for work, she knew, and to broach the troubling question of the rent to be paid to her hosts. And then the words of Adem's poem came back to her:

Between attic and basement
I found this little box
Splinters, holes in memory

Through which the shell flows
Awash in the blood of words
Black sea red sea
As far as love

In her head, she repeated, "Awash in the blood of words," and she saw Hannah looking at her with her characteristic intensity, a look of being distant but at the same time present, far away yet here, a detachment accompanied by indulgence. Bosnia was about to ask her, "Where does your goodness come from?"—from what territory, from what age—and how she was able to hang on to it in today's world of cynicism and disillusionment. But Hannah spoke first, about everything and nothing, about the book she was reading, about the forgiveness the victims of the Shoah could not grant their murderers, because they were dead, those victims, unless there was an eternal, divine criminal court where, by definition, there would be no statute of limitations, and hell would be that Last Judgment pronounced by the one God, single and unique in His word—but she didn't believe in Him, she didn't believe any more. So, after everything she had been through, she had constructed her own criminal court in her heart and had condemned those who did the work of death, physical or psychological, to the obloquy of absence and annihilation—they no longer existed for her, and she no longer thought about them or saw them. And day after day, for all others, she cultivated this thing that could only be called goodness.

It had stopped raining. They went out to the garden and Bosnia said everything that was burning in her heart and her mind that morning. She spoke of her love for Adem, but also of her hopelessness in the face of human corruption, of her infinite affection for her mother, but also of the wounds of losing her father and her friends; she spoke of the rape and of her horror at the prospect of seeing Mumo again, Mumo who was no longer himself; and she spoke of her dream of attending university and of her desire for a child, of her longing to read, to dream, to rest, to waste time. "I'm twenty-six years old, Hannah, and some days, I feel like an old woman, as if I were at least fifty." And she confessed her desire for death, which came back periodically in dreams of vertigo or labyrinths, as if death and the void were pulling her into their annihilating vortex—even though most of the time, she knew she was incapable of taking the irreversible step of killing herself.

They went back inside, and Hannah made more coffee and they continued talking the whole morning. Bosnia also confided her discomfort about money and the debt they owed them. Hannah just laughed and took charge, explaining the situation. Toscan had no progeny and she herself had never had children—"I spent my childbearing years in the camps, without love"—and they wanted nothing more than to help them. Of course, added Hannah, Bosnia could occupy herself with "little translation jobs, so as to keep in touch with the real world." (Later, after discussing it with Toscan, Hannah proposed that Bosnia clean the apartment once a week—"You choose the day." Bosnia answered, "That would be fine, it's a deal," and kissed her. "As for the rest," Hannah said, "take your time, dear, give things time.")

And Hannah told Bosnia about the time fifteen years ago—after she had returned from Israel, which had disappointed her so much, and right after she had been struck by the light of reason and had her "deconversion," her "atheist enlightenment"—she had seen the three holy figures of Yahweh, Allah, and Jesus Christ, with the Father and the Holy Ghost, dying, their light extinguished in the human darkness. How, one day, after she had considered all the prophets and the saints, the virgins and the martyrs, and the characters in all the mythologies of the world—Greek, Latin, Aztec, Hindu, and Innu—and had drawn from them every possible lesson on the unfathomable complexity of human tragedy, that enigmatic intelligence of things, having once illuminated everything, extinguished all light within her and around her, from the stars in the sky to the least twig in the garden, and she realized she had been without real love for such a long time, and without any hope of seeing a change in the course of the world's history or her own, and she felt herself suddenly walking on a ridge between two abysses and she felt dizzy. Lacking even Cioran's recourse of writing a book, she could see only three possible outcomes— none of which pleased her—she could commit suicide (but every suicide scenario horrified her—drowning, hanging, bullet, or drugs, they all repelled her); she could go home and spend the rest of her days doing

NOTHING (but to her, doing NOTHING was much worse, a much more active suffering, than not doing anything, "You understand, Bosnia?"); or she could go dine alone in a big restaurant (and she would see!). She picked the third option. It was in the restaurant that very evening that she had met Toscan, who happened to be in about the same frame of mind as she was. On the restaurant table, the die had been cast, in a way they never could have predicted. And chance had opened another path.

Hardly thinking, they moved towards the piano. Hannah picked up her sheet music and played Liszt's "Bénédiction de Dieu dans la Solitude." Bosnia thought, "It's like making love, you don't need to cry or to laugh, it's the body itself that plays."

After finishing the piece, Hannah asked, "Shall we go and visit Toscan's shop this afternoon?"

XXIV

As they walked up Boulevard du Port-Royal, where Toscan's shop was located, Hannah pointed out the commemorative plaque at No. 31, with the names of Paul Claudel and his sister Camille, who had lived in that house from 1892 to 1896. "You see, when I was a believer—what an odd expression, don't you think?—I was also a fetishist, I would have touched that plaque, because to me that poet so represented the mad hope in a sovereign truth, the certainty of something beyond, something made of light and goodness in the face of the absurdity of the human condition. After the disaster and darkness of Nazism for my people, who for centuries had experienced exile, pogroms, and diasporas, I saw in this poet, as in Nietzsche, a defence of hope, a way of attuning the word to the breath alone, another way of knowing—he went, by a long detour through Greek tragedy, 'to the depths of the definite to find the infinite,' isn't that beautiful? You know, dear, it was the fifties, it was a time when I was reading the Greek tragedies and the Bible, the Old Testament and the New, and many of the great

Western mystics, including—it's strange, but I don't see any contradiction in it—the great Spanish Jewish philosopher of the twelfth century, Abulafia, and his *Seven Ways of the Law*. I still love them all, those believers in the Eternal, I deny nothing of my reading of that time, none of that nourishment I needed to survive. But one day, as I told you, the dark night itself became radiant." Hannah stroked the marble plaque, lovingly acknowledging her vanished past. They continued their walk arm-in-arm, and crossed not far from the little Rue Pascal.

Toscan rose from his workbench to kiss them tenderly. "Did you sleep well? Have a good breakfast? How about a nice cup of coffee?" were his words of greeting. While he busied himself with the coffee in the back of the shop, Bosnia looked around, fascinated by this small place that in some ways reminded her of a workshop of the nineteenth century, or even earlier, it had an almost medieval atmosphere. The room was divided in two by a big oak table gnawed by time, which served as Toscan's workbench. Hanging on the wall or lying on the table were materials and tools for repairing watches—"Watches, but not clocks," Toscan always said when he spoke to the public; "Watches, but not clocks," he repeated every time a new client came in—and those for setting and polishing jewels, and even melting down gold (in the window, Bosnia had noticed a sign: "We buy estate gold. It can be melted down to make jewellery"). Behind the workbench, Toscan practised his trade as a jeweller and goldsmith, and in front of it, he was the salesman for his own jewellery—eighteen-carat gold, cultured pearls, or occasionally, diamonds, which were in the back in a safe. He also sold a few precious and semi-precious gems—amethysts, agates, opals, quartz—the stones alone or set in necklaces, bracelets, brooches, or earrings. Toscan was a true artist, though he called himself a craftsman, and his shop, which at first glance was total chaos, slowly revealed its order to anyone capable of grasping the spirit of the place, which was both inspired and industrious.

Under the sun, which had finally managed to slip through the curtain of rain, the gold sparkled, the gems regained their translucence, and iridescent glints from the fire opal and the sun opal played on the burgundy velvet on which they were displayed, a thousand small movements in a ballet that the delighted Bosnia would have liked to paint. "But you could never achieve this quality of light with paints," she said almost inaudibly, and Hannah answered, as if it went without saying, "That is why we need musicians and poets." Toscan, nodding agreement, served them coffee. They savoured it slowly, in the silence demanded by the beauty and the work around them.

Bosnia was getting ready to explore this Paris that had been the stuff of her dreams for so many years. She would start with her neighbourhood in the fifth, then work her way outward to the adjoining arrondissements, the sixth, the thirteenth, and the fourteenth. She would buy a map for herself, but for the time being she would use the tattered one Hannah had lent her. Today she had set herself an objective: Boulevard St-Germain-des-

Prés, by way of Boulevard du Montparnasse, Boulevard Raspail, and Rue de Rennes. But there was another route she also found enticing: up Boulevard St-Michel, along the Jardin du Luxembourg, and onto Rue de Vaugirard through Place Edmond-Rostand. She hesitated. It bothered her to unfold her map in front of all the passersby, she would rather memorize it and take her chances, even if she got lost, she wanted so much not to be taken for a tourist. "I will never be a tourist anywhere," she said to herself, "I will be an immigrant everywhere, an exile, a wanderer"—and she thought of Le Clézio's *Wandering Star*, which had revealed to her a part of herself that had been nameless until then— "Even if I return to my country, I will be a wandering star that passes, that leaves and then comes back. I am not a tourist, I don't visit, I stay where I pass, I inhabit." She did not open her map in front of passersby, she wanted to melt into the crowd, invisible and anonymous, but perfectly herself, at home or elsewhere, completely there where she was, in total awareness, at home, elsewhere-everywhere. A stranger. Native and non-native everywhere, that's what she was.

Hannah walked with her as far as Rue St-Jacques. Kissing her goodbye, she said, since Bosnia had been silent since the coffee, "I understand you, dear. Wherever you are, cultivate your solitude as your most precious possession. Dinner is at eight tonight. We're celebrating the end of Ramadan. You know, Toscan and I celebrate all the major festivals of the three monotheistic religions, Passover and Easter, Muslim Eid, Christmas. Without really making a decision, we ended up operating on all three calendars." Then she added, dreamily, "Ah, festivals, that is the most beautiful thing the religions have given us!" Slipping a banknote into Bosnia's hand, she laughed a childlike laugh. "Could you take care of the cheese for tonight?" But in Bosnia's hand, there was a lot more than enough for the cheese. She saw Hannah turn and wave before heading down a little street to the right, and Bosnia blew her a kiss back and then saw her disappear like a shadow, a small, slightly stooped woman, but so beautiful, a woman she hadn't known the day before yesterday but already loved. Bosnia felt like sobbing softly, but she let her tears flow inside.

Walking through the streets, she didn't have eyes enough to admire everything there was to see and to buy, the profusion of food in the windows—fruits, cheeses, fresh and prepared meats of all kinds, who could possibly eat all that? And the breads, the pastries, the wines?—in just one street, there was more to eat and drink than in all of Sarajevo. Plus the mountains of books, clothes, jewellery, beauty products—where do they get all the money? She went into two bookstores, did not even dare to treat herself to a book, it was too much, she didn't know how to choose. She went into a clothing shop, a shoe store—when do they wear all these beautiful things? She suddenly felt overwhelmed, bombarded by the abundance, the richness, the luxury, the profusion of goods; it was too much, all too much, and it took away her capacity for contemplation. She thought of Sarajevo as if it were a person, Sarajevo as a little sister who had been disinherited in favour of the big sister, Paris, and she found this absolutely unfair—what secular, profiteering god had contrived this legacy of imbalance, and why? She went and sat down on the stone rim of Fontaine St-Sulpice, no longer wanting to go for coffee or even to the cinema as she had at first imagined, just sitting there, letting herself drift, no longer seeing the passersby, their feet going in all directions, the bags full of purchases strapped on their backs or hanging from their arms.

She saw Sarajevo again as if she were there, she saw her city abandoned to plundering, depression, privation, she remembered the fire and the blood, the dead and wounded bodies, she heard the screams, the weeping, and the death rattles. She thought of the poor books they had had to sacrifice one by one, and she looked all around her and realized that on Place St-Sulpice alone, there were enough trees, doors, and window frames to fuel fires in Sarajevo for ten years of siege. She saw the home of her childhood, the one that had been looted and burned down, and decided to go into the damp darkness of the church. She was surprised to find that someone was playing the organ in the peaceful silence there. Sitting alone in the midst of the calm and the emptiness, she found herself back in her forest, alone and wild, and among the columns of this theatre of worship as then among the trees, a phrase from the Bosnian writer Velibor Čolić came back to her: "Then they climbed back into the tank and once again ploughed with its treads the garden of my childhood." She was a thousand miles from the garden of her childhood, but the mere memory of it, even though it was sad, gave rise to the extraordinary joy she always felt when luxuriance was combined with simplicity.

On her way back, already anticipating the celebration, to which even Stefan had been invited, she wondered, "What is the source of the evil that since the beginning of human time, has produced war and injustice?"

XXV

THE EVENING CELEBRATION marking the end of Ramadan (which, in any case, no one observed) was filled with new developments. Everyone arrived around seven, and Hannah greeted them cheerfully. She gave Bosnia a letter from her Mamouni, which she would read later in her bedroom and then reread to Adem, her voice thick with emotion. As for Adem, he had had a productive day, first at UNESCO, where he and Bosnia would be able to get translation contracts, and then with Stefan at the law faculty. But he still had to obtain piles of applications and other papers from the Préfecture de Police and the temporary consular services that had been set up in the capitals of countries taking in Bosnian refugees. Since the Dayton Agreement,* there had been no embassy to represent nationals of Bosnia-Herzegovina—especially not the Belgrade embassy. Fortunately, the Bosnian refugee centre existed to facilitate things for them. "I

---

* In 1995, under the auspices of the international community, this agreement consolidated the de facto partition of Bosnia-Herzegovina and the Bosnian Serb Republic (Republika Srpska).

won't start my classes at the university until September," he announced to the gathering, "but I'm going to audit some courses." Meanwhile, he had to run from one department to another, showing his credentials each time, enduring cool receptions, callous treatment, and even rudeness or outright rejection from various officials and bureaucrats. He wondered why this unpleasantness and lack of goodwill was so prevalent among employees in this society of abundance, where people had every reason to be satisfied. He reflected, "Every country has its forms of war. Here, it appears, they are scattered among everyday occurrences like microscopic insects—but will the thousands of little wars end up in one big one?" The idea depressed him. Sometimes, all it took to boost his morale was a single smile or a word of encouragement—"Don't worry, things will be fine!" with a wink to express support—or the spontaneous, joyful solidarity that arose among "claimants" waiting in the interminable lines or on uncomfortable benches, with their crumpled numbers, in grey, icy rooms, and then he would say to himself that after all, these ordinary hardships were nothing compared to the horrors of war, and that, while this wasn't paradise on earth, peace was better than what he had known in his country.

Feeling rather dejected all the same, Adem told how in one office, when he had dared to remark on the unwarranted brusqueness, the employee had retorted, almost shouting so everyone would hear, "If you're not happy, go back where you came from!" Adem was outraged, but he kept his mouth shut; he felt crushed and humiliated, even though, when facing a murderous enemy, he had always been able to take "an eye for an eye and a tooth for a tooth," had always been able to turn an attack back on itself and give as good as he got. But in front of that employee, and surrounded by unsympathetic onlookers, he felt shameful, a usurper, a thief of space, needy. Hearing this story, Toscan, who often remained silent, described his own arrival in France, just after the 1939–1945 war, his flight from Yugoslavia following the deaths in the Nazi camps of almost his entire family, who were well-known Communists, and of his young bride, Valida. He told of his father and mother, uncles, aunts, cousins, and friends, and of living in hiding with his young brother, Milovan, and how wrenching it was when they were separated—the uprooting and the pain had still not healed in either of them, they didn't need to say anything to each other, they knew it, they felt it, on the telephone or when they wrote each other, it was as if each brother read the thoughts of the other, as if each of them had buried, deep in his heart in an identical little box he never opened any more, the same recollections drawn from living memory. "To survive, to simply continue to live," said Toscan pensively, and then, speaking to Adem, "Even meanness, my boy, store it deep inside you. When you're working as a lawyer, it will help you understand wrongdoers. To help the victims, you have to understand the perpetrators. You always know that little box is there, my boy, you never open it, but it's there, sealed, what matters is knowing it's still there."

Hannah put on her favourite CD, *Tantôt rouge tantôt bleu*, Mona Heftre singing Rezvani. She said, "Adem, dear, this song, which is my citizen's anthem, is for you":

> *I am no one's son*
> *I am from no country*
> *I belong with those men*
> *Who love the earth like a fruit.*

They listened in silence. From time to time, Hannah sang along in her frail but true mezzo—she knew the refrain and verses of all the songs by heart.

The telephone rang. It was Sophie, calling from Lille. She talked to everyone, but Stefan was the one she told all her news. When her parents saw her arrive with her meagre baggage—she had left behind all the furnishings, the linens and bedding, the pots and pans, and other household goods they had paid for, in that apartment that had become a prison—when they heard the story of her life as a slave under the abuse of her brute of a husband, of the arrival of Mirsad's cousin and his lover, who had become her friends and accomplices in her escape, of her meeting with Stefan and the trip to Provence, of the happiness she had regained with her three friends, her mother could not hold back a flood of tears, and took her in her arms, saying, "My poor darling, why didn't you call us?" Her father became enraged and started making plans to go with her to Lyon, where, with his contacts, he would find a good lawyer and they would sue that bastard for unlawful confinement and abuse, have him convicted, and recover the property—"Oh, the punishment will fit the crime, either that damn Mirsad will spend years in prison, or he'll be returned to his miserable country, or both— we'll show him!" When Sophie told them about Stefan and said she wanted to go back to Paris to study at the Beaux-Arts and share an apartment with him, her father's fury rose to new heights, while her mother wept even harder. Her father screamed, "First you chose a torturer and now you're going to move in with a queer? No way, never, on my father's honour, do you hear me? Never!"

"I should never have told you Stefan was gay, I thought you were more open, Papa." Sophie found within herself a source of supreme calm. She went right up to her father, who was usually so affectionate, and adopted the loving tone she had used with him since she was very little, and explained to him everything she knew about homosexuality, saying that it wasn't a defect, and she told him of her affection and esteem for Stefan. "Come what may, I will love him until the end of my days," she said and told him she did not want to make love now with any man, and hadn't for a long time, she had suffered so much in her cage in Lyon, and she made him see that she would, in fact, be protected with Stefan, who "wouldn't want to screw me." "Don't talk like that," her father said, kissing her. "Love is very beautiful, you know. We'll help you."

The upshot of the long day of reunion with her parents was that Sophie had accepted her father's divorce strategy and agreed to stay in Lille for a year.

After all, they had agreed to her plans for the Beaux-Arts, give and take. Of course, she could go to Paris as often as she wanted. "You're of age and vaccinated," said her father. "And poor darling, she has suffered so much," added her mother, blowing her nose, "and you can invite your friend Stefan, we'll welcome him, we're not fascists or reactionaries." That evening, in the bedroom of her girlhood, to which she had made an emotional return, her mother came to talk to her. She learned that Sophie was pregnant and immediately stopped crying and regained her composure, and, taking control, formulated the plan for the abortion, with the understanding, of course, that her father would never know. Afterwards, they hugged, crying in each other's arms. "Oh, I would have loved to be a grandmother!" said her mother.

The letter was the first Bosnia had received from her mother since she had left Bosnia-Herzegovina. She had read it before dinner and left it upstairs in her room. Now that she was alone with Adem and they were sitting comfortably side by side on the bed looking out on the patch of clear sky outlined by the dormer window, she wanted to read it to him. She opened up the lined paper folded in four, with the old-fashioned writing that she always found touching, and she read it out loud:

> *My little Sabaheta, I miss you, but I want you to be happy there in France and to follow your own path, may Allah protect you! The same*

thing for Adem, give him my love. I am fine and my friend Liliana is too. Her two older daughters wanted her to leave Herzegovina with them and go to Italy. But she told them, I'm staying, I'm fine here. The daughters made a fuss and she told them, you're not doing this for love, it's selfishness, you just want what's best for you. In the end, Milovan resolved it. And the daughters went back to Italy. Milovan is more and more our good friend. He comes and plays cards with us. Or all three of us go walking in the streets. It's very sad to see the city torn to pieces by the shelling. To make a living, Liliana and I have set up a sewing workshop in our kitchen. But the saddest thing, my poor little girl, is your brother Mumo. They changed him in Arabia. He was in a Koranic school, I forget the name of it. They taught him vengeance. He has hatred in his heart. He'd like me to wear a veil. He has hatred in his eyes. If your father saw him, he would be sad. I don't want to see him any more, it's too painful. I don't recognize him any more. Last night, I dreamed he was on my belly, he had a man's face and a beard, but at the same time, he was a baby. I went out to get medicine and I got lost in the streets. When I finally found my way again and returned home, he wasn't there any more. I cried and I woke up. Liliana says not to think about him any more. We all feel too guilty, we mothers. Couldn't you come back for a little while, maybe a week? Maybe you could make him come to his senses better than I can. I hold you close to my heart, my child. Best regards to those good people who are looking after you. They will be rewarded in heaven, Insh'Allah. Good luck and all the best to Adem in his studies.

Your mama

PS. Milovan says that if you come with Adem, he'll pay your fare and you could stay with him. Here, with Liliana, there's no room now, but you'll come and visit every day, Allah Akbar.

Bosnia folded the letter and put it back on the night table. She was moved, but fatigue kept her from finding the words to talk. She huddled against Adem, and they talked about this and that and made plans to return to Sarajevo for a few days, probably in the spring, when the hills are so beautiful. Then, without thinking about it first, without even knowing why, Bosnia asked Adem, "Would you be there with me the first time I meet Mumo?" Adem, half asleep, agreed.

XXVI

DECEMBER HAD BEEN VERY GREY, but that morning, the sun came up, a big ball of yellow yarn under the clouds, which gradually dissipated. Bosnia watched the big circle of the sky, her nose pressed against the window, wondering how she should spend her day, vacillating between the desire to curl up in bed with a good book—these days, having registered as an auditor in a philosophy course at the Sorbonne, she was reading "thinkers rather than artists," as she told everyone—and the desire to go out and see an exhibition or a film. She went to the cinema almost every day, sometimes with Hannah, who was a real film buff and was introducing her to the seventh art—together they had seen many of the films shown at the Cinémathèque and the art and experimental cinemas. But sometimes Adem would go with her when he had a free morning, which was rare, and she savoured every instant of these excursions, when the two of them sat riveted to the movement on the screen, feeling their love amid the muffled sounds in the darkness as nowhere else. The last film they had seen together was *Ulysses' Gaze* by

Angelopoulos, and they had gone out into the street afterward, hand in hand, mad with a shared joy, telling each other that after that inspired film, they would never see life the same way again, or even the city, which they barely recognized.

It was the sun that won the day. She would go out. That day she felt an irrepressible need to be alone, and when that happened, there was nothing in the world that could distract her from this command of the heart, neither the noise nor the crowds of passersby along the way, nothing could take her out of herself or get into her, she lived within her solitude as in a house she had built for herself deep in the forest or facing the great open sea. But in fact, she had been born in that little house, and all she had done over the years was add rooms, doors, windows. During the war, she had dug a long basement with her bare hands by the light of a weak lantern—she never sought to return, she wanted no more of that haunted solitude, but lately, in her night dreams, she would find herself there again in spite of herself, sometimes waking with her body pressed to the sticky wall and vile insects clinging to her hair. She had just had one of those nights, had been vaguely aware of Adem getting up, preparing his things, kissing her, and leaving, and then had found herself, against her will, going back down the path of sleep through those gloomy cellars, and then a scream had propelled her into the bright morning and she had found herself facing the sun, her nose pressed to the window, her soul wavering between the beauty of the day and the scraps of nightmares still floating in the air. It was decided:

neither the book, nor the cinema, nor the church where she sometimes took refuge and listened to free concerts, no, she would go out into the sun, she would walk and she would think, because for a while now, one nagging question had been clouding her happiness: "What am I doing with my life?"

Of course, she was young, but although she told herself "I'm only twenty-six, nearly twenty-seven," she was also thinking, "Before long, I'll be thirty, and then forty, and if I go on like this, I'll have done nothing with my life." Looking in the mirror, she found herself young and pretty, and Adem had told her, "You're very beautiful, the most beautiful of all"—but inside, in her secret mirror, there was already an old woman who had accomplished nothing, and yet who had dreamed a lot before the war and then, especially, fighting in the forest at her father's side, had envisioned the greatest of destinies for herself. To reassure herself, she constantly reminded herself of simple things, such as her studies, which the war had interrupted and which she would go back to as soon as some unforeseen path opened up, showing her the true way. She still wanted to become a doctor of the mind, and had a desire to have a child, a desire that had been put aside temporarily—in their uncertain circumstances, it would be insane for her and Adem to take the risk of bringing a child into the world, and what a world! In the name of no-God! It would be irresponsible to take that risk, they both said—and for now she sensibly took her contraceptives. But sometimes she worried about having to make room one day in her little house deep in the forest or facing the great open sea. Would she find the space for another being, even a very small one, and one who would have to first pass through the abode of her own body? When the time came, would she be able to enlarge the domain of her solitude? Or would bearing and raising a child mean making a garden between two retreats, as many gardens as there would be children, so that life would consist of opening up a domain deep in the forest or facing the great open sea? But Bosnia never talked to Adem about all this. Why not? She wanted to think about that, too.

The day would be cool, she would dress warmly and walk in the sun, always on the sunny side of the street, she would perhaps go to a park, she needed trees and vegetation and, missing the meadows and pastures and woods of her childhood, she at least wanted to smell the air of the earth, to feel the humus of the frozen ground cracking under the heat of the sun, she needed to reconnect with the soil in the city oasis, to hear the winter birds, those sedentary species whose loyalty to one homeland nevertheless had not prevented them from flying or from singing out in a language that had come from elsewhere a long time ago.

She heard the sound of Hannah's piano reverberating through the house. In the mornings, Hannah practised her scales, chords, and arpeggios and some Czerny studies, her "warm-up exercises," to keep in shape, which gave the apartment an atmosphere that reminded Bosnia of the most beautiful times in her childhood, when she and her mother would go and spend several weeks of the summer in Romania with her grandparents, when the whole household of young uncles and aunts, all of them musicians, would play the piano and violin, sing, and dance, while the grandfather, with his moustache and the beret he always wore, listened, smiling benignly amid wreaths of pipe smoke. And a phrase fell from the heavens to Bosnia's ears: "They may speak of the wings of love / But death flies a hundred times higher." Where did these words come from, just when she was seeing again the faces of her mother's Romanian family, all of them so happy in her memory, all of them departed, over the years, to the other side of life? Where did the two lines come from when she was luxuriating in nostalgia, carried away by Hannah's piano? Then, as she was going downstairs to the kitchen to make herself a nice cup of coffee, the phrase found its home. It had come from her Russian poetry class in high school, from a poem by Osip Mandelstam, written in 1917 and dedicated to Anna Akhmatova, and it had excerpted itself and inscribed itself in the sky of memory, a star shining in the night of death.

"When I go by the living room, I'll kiss Hannah and I'll ask her, as someone who has experienced the genocide of her people and the Nazi and Soviet camps, and who is not far from death—but I'll suggest that delicately—where does she reap her joy, from what soil or in what clearing, and on what path did she one day come upon it?"

Hannah came over to have a cup of coffee with Bosnia, who, by way of a greeting, repeated Mandelstam's verse for Akhmatova: "They may speak of the wings of love / But death flies a hundred times higher." Then she talked a little about her Romanian family, but she did not ask her questions about happiness and joy. She was already outside when she remembered them.

She had left for the Jardin des Plantes, after all, it was so near the apartment, and she needed calm and serenity, to sit among the pansies, mauve, white, and yellow, the only flowers that braved the winter and never seemed to die. As always when she came this way, she passed the Great Mosque of Paris. She did not want to go into it, ever, she was determined to flee everything here that would bring back malevolent memories. And if it had been an Orthodox church, she would have behaved the same way—since the war, that religion was for her a hell of savagery and tortures that defied all imagination. When she thought of the horrors experienced by her family, when, in a flash, sometimes right in the middle of a film, a conversation, or a book, fragments of obscene images rose again to consciousness—no, she did not want to, she fled those so-called sacred places that for her were branded with the weapons and tools of death.

She walked along all the pathways of the Jardin des Plantes and finally sat down beside her favourite one, the one where the sun stayed the longest. She let her mind drift, following the ebb and flow of life—birds, leaves, petals moving under the slanting rays, no solitary strollers, only crows shaking themselves under the sun in a puddle as black as they were, playing—it wasn't every day they found such an ocean under the blue sky—and then one of them leaving the group to painstakingly bury a crust of bread under a clump of earth.

And then, all of a sudden, sitting dreamily on her bench, no longer thinking about anything in particular, especially not about the general meaning she should give to her life, she had a feeling of certainty as clear as the ball of sun that was about to disappear behind the buildings on Rue Buffon, a feeling that she must return to Sarajevo as soon as possible, not in the spring, no, immediately after the holidays, because it was impossible sooner, they had promised Hannah and Toscan they would celebrate Christmas all together— even Sophie would come, since her parents had long ago planned a voyage to the sunny climes of Egypt— but now, sitting on this bench in the Jardin des Plantes, she felt a sense of urgency, the pressing call of Mamouni and Bosnia-Herzegovina mingled with an uneasy desire to see Mumo again without delay and have a heart-to-heart talk with this brother she had loved so much and still believed she would be able to cherish again.

On her way back, she saw Adem coming up Rue du Fer à Moulin. She rushed into his arms and asked breathlessly, "Do you want to come with me to Sarajevo right after the holidays?"

XXVII

BOSNIA TIPTOED INTO THE ROOM, which was all white, even Hannah was white, her hair, her face, her hands, and her nightgown, and the bright sunshine filtering through the half-closed blinds flooded the room with a surreal light, as if she were moving through a space lined in velvet. Nothing was moving, not even Hannah's face or body—"Oh my God, I hope she's not dead!" Bosnia went closer, saw that Hannah was breathing, sat down in the chair between the window and the bed, and amid the great silence of illness, thought of the fright they had had when, in the evening on December 20, Hannah had collapsed on the dining room floor, and of their controlled haste, their forced calm, even though they all could have screamed in terror. She remembered Toscan taking Hannah's pulse, Adem running to get a cold compress, herself dialling 15 for the ambulance, Toscan tangled up in the phone cord, trying to explain, and finally, the ambulance heading towards Cochin Hospital, with Hannah and Toscan in it, while she and Adem stayed at the apartment riveted to the telephone and cleared up, did the dishes, and had another coffee. And Bosnia remembered the shards of china on the floor, because when she fell, Hannah had taken her cup of herbal tea with her. When Toscan returned very early in the morning, they learned that Hannah had angina and tachycardia. "She'll pull through, she's sleeping now, she needs a lot of rest," the doctor had said.

Hannah was sleeping peacefully. She would have to stay in the hospital a few more days. It was December 24 and, in accordance with Hannah's wishes, they had decided to go ahead with the Christmas Eve *reveillon* despite her absence. Toscan had closed up shop. The plans they had made at the last minute in a "family council," as he called it, had been submitted to Hannah, so that all she had to do was give her assent and smile, saying, "Children, enjoy yourselves just as if I were there." They were making jokes, but it was all pretense, it just wouldn't be the same. Bosnia would therefore spend the afternoon with Hannah, while Toscan and Adem would do the shopping and Stefan and Sophie the cleaning, as decreed by Toscan. Bosnia again remembered the shards of china on the floor, she was constantly superimposing that scene on one of exploding shells, just as the memory of Hannah's ashen body on the floor endlessly took her back to the bodies of her two friends hit by shell fragments. To keep herself from sinking into morbid memories, she went over the menu they had put together for the party with Hannah the day before, while Toscan was at the shop. "Children, you should do everything exactly the same for Toscan. I'll explain it to you." First there would be the ritual foie gras with champagne, followed by oysters, the flat kind from Cancale, because they had taken one of the most beautiful trips of their lives there. Next there would be a capon with three-fruit stuffing—"The three fruits are pitted prunes, crushed chestnuts, and grated apples"—and she had explained to them in detail how to stuff the bird, how to sew it up, and in which drawer to find the needle and cotton string, and then how to brush the skin, how and at what temperature to roast the bird, and how to baste it. "One day you'll have a family, you have to know how to cook," she told Bosnia and Adem, her appointed chefs. "You'll also need a little salad after the bird, vegetables are good for you." As for the wines and cheeses, it was understood that Toscan would take care of them, and Stefan and Sophie had offered to bring dessert. "Ask Toscan, he'll tell you that you have to have a Yule log, and which one and where you have to buy it."

Toscan had begged Doctor B., Hannah's physician, to let them organize a very small party for her in the hospital at around eight o'clock in the evening: "Just a few oysters, four or five, which we'll open at home and bring to her room on ice, and we'll drink a glass of Condrieu with her, she loves it, no champagne, Doctor, I agree, it would excite her, and certainly no foie gras, not this year anyway." Doctor B. had given his approval and had even agreed to let the patient taste a slice of capon breast with a little stuffing on the afternoon of the twenty-fifth: "It could only do her good—but no sauce, and no wine this time, you understand?" and they exchanged season's greetings.

(That evening, Toscan explained to them what Condrieu meant to him and Hannah. It was there, in the town of Condrieu itself, that they had spent their honeymoon, in 1958, to be exact, after their marriage at the town hall of the fourteenth arrondissement, where Hannah lived at the time—"A Republican marriage," Toscan pointed out. And it was in the Condrieu region of the Rhône valley that they had discovered the joys of wine, tasting Côte Rôtie, Crozes-Hermitage, Gigondas, St-Joseph, Châteauneuf-du-Pape, and so many others. "And then we slept in Vienne and then under the Dentelles de Montmirail, and we went as far as Mont Ventoux and enjoyed its vineyards. Oh! Children, not to know the love of wine, is not to know love itself." Toscan fell silent, thinking of that wedding trip among the vineyards and of Hannah, his love, whom he did not want to lose, ever. Before going to bed, he said, "You'll see tomorrow, you'll taste it. Good night, children. Lock up before you go to bed." Bosnia and Adem watched him head toward his bedroom, and his bed, where he would breathe in the smell of Hannah till the next day.)

Doctor B. entered the room, went over to Hannah, took her pulse, and wished her merry Christmas, which woke her up. "Oh, I must have dozed off," she responded. "Come and give me a kiss, dear. I feel better. I'm going to be fine, you know. The journey to eternity will be for another time." "Yes, but if you want to stay in this world, you'll have to behave yourself," the doctor said in a half-authoritative, half-affectionate tone. He went over to Bosnia and held out his hand. "Is this your daughter?" "She's a bit too young for that," answered Hannah. The doctor continued, "You'll have to behave yourself. That means plenty of rest. A little cooking, walks, piano, but no housecleaning, no shopping—you should never carry bags or heavy packages. You should have help around the house and I insist that you have someone do your shopping. I've spoken to your husband about it." He continued in the same vein, with gentle firmness. "Well I accept all that, Doctor, but no one's going to stop me from going to the Sunday market on Rue Mouffetard. Across from St-Médard Church, behind the Arab fruit and vegetable stands, there's always a choir and everyone sings, old, young, and in-between, and I sing with them. We're accompanied by an accordion, it's beautiful, it revitalizes me every time. Last Sunday, they sang, we sang, 'La Romance de Paris,' 'Frou Frou,' and 'Que reste-t-il de nos amours?' There was even a fat American man who sang an Italian opera aria, I forget which one, and it was very moving." Doctor B. smiled, "Of course you can sing, but no shopping, no carrying heavy packages." They continued chatting for a little while. After he had left, Hannah told Bosnia the "young man" looked a lot like her older brother, Serge, who had been gassed in Auschwitz; he had just turned twenty-seven, and as a matter of fact, he had been studying medicine.

"Come sit close, we'll talk," she said to Bosnia. Bosnia moved her chair closer and took Hannah's hand, which she found cold. She pulled the sheet up over Hannah's arms, raised the head of the bed a little, fluffed the pillows, gently brushed Hannah's curly white hair, and kissed her on the forehead. Without really thinking about it first, she asked her if she thought it possible that she and Adem would still love each other when they were old, and particularly, but this embarrassed her a little and she apologized for it, "Can you still have pleasure, I mean sexually, when you're old?" Hannah smiled and answered, "Yes, of course, my dear, maybe not so often, and less frenetically, but I would say it's better, deeper, more intense and gentler, you feel things better, you see. I'd compare it to grape vines: the greater the age of the vines, the lower their yield, wine makers say. But they produce magnificent wine of unparalleled depth." She added, "Cherish each other, you two, you're wonderful, you deserve it, you've suffered a lot and you are still feeling the pain of past suffering. But you will find ways to staunch the wounds, you both have the capacity to heal."

Bosnia did not want to tire Hannah out, but she sensed her need to talk. She had no daughters or granddaughters, or even a niece, and her goddaughter had been killed at the age of two in the Holocaust. Bosnia asked questions that drew on what she thought of as Hannah's wisdom and joy. "Ah, wisdom, my little one, I don't know. But joy, yes, it comes from the great fatigue, the exhaustion, I would say, that one feels in the face of the inhumanity we experienced during the war. It's rather strange, rather difficult to explain, but the horror did not spoil the beauty of the world. You see, I had gone so deep into sadness and despair that in order to go on living, all I could do was try to use the light from above to reach the peaks. As if there had to be a counterpart to the Nazi barbarity, something higher than humanity to cling to, at least long enough to get back on an even keel, to learn to breathe again in the free air. One day, something clicked in my mind. It happened in the middle of the Mediterranean, on the boat taking me to Israel with a lot of Jews who had survived the camps, many of whom were filled with despair. I was on deck, I was thirty years old, with no plans for the future, only the past weighing on the uncertain present. We were sailing with our backs to the sun, our eyes turned to the east on which we had all set our hopes. I knew no one among my travelling companions, I was in such total solitude I could not even express it, I realized that all the people I had loved were dead, absolutely all of them, family, friends, lovers, all, and I decided to recall each one of them, face, body, and gestures, I spoke each name accompanied by the sound of the lapping of the waves on the side of the ship, I didn't cry, it was as if I was officiating at a solemn ceremony for a whole nation of the dead, whose names had become a sacred chant, and as if they, the lost beings, were finally letting themselves be rocked by the music of the waves. That was when everything turned upside-down. I had suffered my fill, I felt like a spring that had run dry, that has to be filled or else the earth all around it will die, but filled with what, I asked myself, with anger or a desire for revenge? I had tried that and it led nowhere, I could have given in to raw despair, the delirium of madness, or suicide, but something stopped me, I don't know what. And in that fraction of an instant, my life was turned inside-out like a glove and I made a choice, alone with my dead, whose names resonated among the waves of the Mediterranean. It was as clear as that blue sky above, it was a choice I would never abandon, the choice of joy—don't ask where it came from.

"Of course, my dear, when we landed in Israel, a refugee among refugees, I turned, like many of my compatriots, to psychoanalysis—I needed to lay a foundation for that impulsive joy, to visit the house from top to bottom and survey the garden, even though it had been destroyed, and the whole neighbourhood. To carry on the work to the ends of the earth, you know …

"You see, it is not surprising that my people, the people of the Shoah, produced one of the greatest healers of all time—have you heard of Freud? My dear, humanity will one day have to understand that peoples, particularly those who have suffered the most, must produce their own healers and free themselves from absolute, all-powerful gods. Otherwise, the wheel of disaster will continue to turn. But perhaps tragedy is our earthly lot. If that's the case, we have to embrace joy even more intensely. Oh, my dear! We must drink to beauty, drink to life."

Hannah mimed raising a glass, and Bosnia did likewise. They drank in silence from invisible goblets in the dim light of the hospital room, to the clacking of the nurses' plastic-soled clogs, they drank to their shared commitment to joy although the reasons escaped them.

Then Bosnia left so that Hannah could rest. In a few hours, she would be surrounded by people at the "little party" with the oysters from Cancale and the Condrieu. Afterwards, the rest of them would walk home together on Boulevard du Port-Royal under the stars, to the "big party" where they would miss Hannah dreadfully. They would look at the crescent moon shining above the dome of Val-de-Grâce, and each of them would wonder, "Will Hannah come back to us better, and when?"

XXVIII

AFTER A JOURNEY marked by turbulence over the Alps and checks by suspicious customs agents, Bosnia and Adem finally saw the glass door open, and spotted Milovan in the midst of an impatient crowd, his smile radiant although he was thinner and a bit stooped and had big circles under his eyes, having borne the depression and privation of recent months, a time of trials and tribulations for post-war Bosnia. He had come to welcome them at Ljubljana Airport in his old wreck of a car (no one but the SFOR soldiers and humanitarian workers from the international NGOs had decent vehicles, except for the lucky and resourceful few), he had crossed Croatia, stopping at the home of an old friend from military service when they were twenty, during the time of united Yugoslavia, and noting that the moral, political, and economic misery of the Croatians was similar to their own, but he had been happy to have a chance to speak the Serbo-Croatian language of his youth and to discuss things as they had enjoyed doing in the old days, before the ethnic and religious madness took hold of men of power, rekindled ancestral hatreds, and became pandemic in the Balkans.

They rushed into each other's arms, Milovan repeating over and over, "I'm so happy to see you again, my children," and stroking their heads, Bosnia drowning in the flood of tears she was clumsily trying to hide, and Adem silent. "We'll head back to Sarajevo tomorrow, kids. Tonight we'll rest. I found a wonderful inn in a little village not far from here, and I've reserved two rooms. We'll eat there tonight, we'll have a nice bottle of wine and we'll talk." Bosnia and Adem couldn't have asked for anything more; they had so much to talk about with him, but where to begin? The war already seemed far behind, just so many memories, like a nightmare the three of them had shared and from which they'd awakened with the same wounds, the same shared dead, the same attempts to forget, which from time to time were successful, and the same need to talk when they were "alone among themselves," as all the survivors said. And this was the first time the three of them were alone among themselves, in that muddled, indefinite space where an allusion led to endless stories and sometimes a single word was enough to set off the epic of which they were the heroes—their dead rejoining them in the often-repeated chronicle, for only among them did their dead return from the nether regions to become living beings again, there with their words, their fears, their songs. And all those people who had not been carried away with them on that ship of war that sailed on tides of blood under lightning from the heavens would, whatever they might think or do, forever be strangers. When they were alone among themselves, be it back at home or far off on foreign soil, they once again, through the magic of sharing the same events that had been promoted to the rank of high adventure by their shared misery, became allies in a shared space of citizenship, and others, all others, regardless of whether they had been born here or elsewhere, were strangers— unless those others, like Hannah and Toscan during the 1939–1945 war, had lived through a similar horror in their flesh.

They talked first about Hannah and Toscan, and Bosnia and Adem couldn't say enough—so much love, so much goodness, how lucky they were to be treated like the children of the house; they saw the poverty, the isolation of other Bosnian refugees they met in France, they could have experienced the same rejection, the same despair—and they could tell Milovan of the guilt they felt sometimes at being so fortunate, so "privileged." And then they told him about their stay in Lyon, their meeting Sophie—and her situation—and then Stefan, who had helped them get translation work and register at the university, what a great friend he was, "He was still himself. You know, Milovan, that he lost his Croat lover during the war, tortured and murdered?" Milovan, at the wheel, raced along the little country road with the joy of a man reunited with his children. They told him about Hannah's angina attack, the little party in the hospital, the "impeccable care in French hospitals," the big party, the friends, the menu, the wines, the extraordinary love of Hannah and Toscan for each other and for them. "Oh, my children, that was the best thing that could have happened to you! Toscan and I were always close, but Hannah, I don't really know very well. This is wonderful, wonderful, kids! Don't feel guilty about being happy now. When life is finally fair, you have to thank it, to acknowledge it very quietly." And Milovan began humming a tune that brought back vague memories, far-off memories of childhood that the war had smothered along with so many people and things that were gone forever.

"Forever," said Adem to himself, but out loud, and everyone knew why he'd said it. Everyone was aware that the burning topic of Mumo had not yet been broached, and that he was the reason Mamouni was so unhappy—"But fortunately she has her friend with her!"—and also the reason Milovan was so anxious, as they were to learn that evening at dinner. "Oh, madness is as frightening as war, maybe even more so," Milovan would say, before kissing them, when they parted for the night at the door of their room.

On the smooth road through Slovenia, driving across the plain along cultivated fields so perfect they looked as if they were in a painting, through tidy villages, past well-ordered houses and farms, each town with its protective little stone church, everything calling to mind a novel in which destiny dictates a happy ending, Bosnia, who had wanted to sit in the back "to think better," even while listening attentively, wondered why Slovenia had escaped the carnage, having managed, at the beginning of the disturbances in Yugoslavia in 1991, to declare independence without violence and without any retaliation from the central government in Belgrade. "Are the Orthodox Serbs less bothered by Catholics than by the Muslims of Bosnia or Kosovo?" she reflected, "After all, they're all Christians." Before dozing off, nestled in the conversation of those two she loved so much, she wondered, "Good God, why did the Ottomans ever have to come to the Balkans?"

The inn was a wonder of order and beauty and their room was very comfortable, but rather austere, which they weren't used to. They had a huge, ultra-modern bathroom, the biggest bed they had ever seen, a sofa and two chairs, and an enormous brick fireplace, which unfortunately they could not use. But they could at least dream of spending weeks there, especially since there was a work table facing the window that looked out on a neatly pruned grove of trees, which gave Bosnia, for the first time in her life, a desire to write her life story. That was what she told Adem, and he took her in his arms, and they could not let go of each other, and before their dinner appointment in the inviting dining room they had glimpsed as they passed, they rolled onto the bed and made love as they hadn't since that time in Marseille beside the inlet, in the salty foam, up there among the gentle echoes of the mistral.

They went and knocked on Milovan's door at the agreed time, their arms laden with gifts from Hannah and Toscan (they also had presents for Mamouni, and even for Mumo): foie gras, duck rillettes, smoked salmon, chocolate, and a surprise—an ingot of gold from Toscan, which Bosnia had hidden in her backpack, rolled up in an old T-shirt; there was less risk of searches for her, since young men were always suspect. They had drinks in the room, champagne brought by the young people, who had also brought four bottles of Rhône wine Toscan had selected from his cellar—they'd got the bottles through customs as if by magic, they'd had the good luck to get a customs agent who was a wine lover. They chatted and laughed, the bubbles carrying them into the sweet sphere of intoxication. There would be plenty of time later for serious things. By tacit agreement, they were putting them off for now.

That time came at dinner. The portrait Milovan gave them of Mumo was devastating. He had no word but madness to describe that "young man nobody understands any more." Even his mother did not recognize her son in this person so consumed by hatred. "Fortunately she has her friend Liliana with her. If she were alone, I think you would have found her back in the asylum, the poor dear. He has even become violent with her, because she refuses to wear the veil and hardly ever goes to the mosque any more. And he became violent with Liliana, because she's Orthodox and Christian and an 'infidel.' He hasn't hit them, but he has really frightened them, he's threatened them. Your mother called me after he'd left, she was shaken, crying. I went to see them right away and she asked if I could do something. I met with your brother at his place, in the suburbs of Sarajevo, he lives in a rundown apartment with some 'Arabs' he met in Saudi Arabia. They talk about jihad, they have weapons, they are training as well as they can in Bosnia, hiding from the

SFOR soldiers. They told me all this because I was a commander during the war, and they wanted me to join them. I listened, powerless, to the speeches of these young fighters, they want holy war, want to wipe all non-believers, Christians and Jews, off the face of the earth. They were brainwashed in the Koranic school and the military camp in Saudi Arabia, they have hatred on their lips and hatred in their hearts, they despise women, they want their absolute submission, 'all veiled,' they say, and 'stoned when they deserve it.'

"I knew that Mumo had been horribly tortured by the Chetniks during his long months in prison. I thought I could read between the lines that he had been raped many times—perhaps mutilated. Thinking about it over the last few weeks, I've come to believe that his tormentors infected him with hatred and death where normally the body takes pleasure. My children, perhaps I'm expressing clumsily what I think I understood. And when I tried to talk with him alone, one day when I had him come to my place, he made all kinds of speeches that didn't make any sense to me. That's what's called delirium, I think, I talked about him with a doctor friend. It was frightening to listen to, I felt he was dangerous, I don't really know why. All I asked of him was not to see his mother any more, and he at least agreed to that. Your mama was devastated at first, and then she pulled herself together with Liliana's help and mine. I have to say she has finally accepted that she can't do anything about this. She no longer wants to see her son for now, as if every visit made the wound in her heart grow bigger. My dear Bosnia, if anyone can change the situation, it's you, you were so close to each other, like twins, as your mama said, you absolutely must see him."

They went on talking for a long time. Bosnia had barely picked at her food, and had drunk a little too much for what she had eaten. She felt cold, as she did when she was facing an ordeal, and she was dizzy. Before Adem put his arm around her shoulders and helped her up the stairs, she just had time to ask, "Tell me, why does this rage and madness always happen to guys?"

XXIX

THE TRIP TO SARAJEVO was sad for Bosnia, who preferred once again to sit alone in the back, looking out at the dark landscape shrouded in thick winter fog. She was feeling down, but she found some comfort in listening to her two companions chatting about this and that. This morning, they were talking politics, each presenting his view of the situation, but they at least agreed on one thing: Bosnia-Herzegovina, having given birth to peace with the help of the forceps of the international community, was suffering from post-partum depression. Milovan and Adem did not recognize this dark offspring that had given rise to disenchantment, a tragic child no one understood or knew what to do with—the war had given them a vocabulary of extraordinary richness, but now in this state of depression, words failed them. Between discussions, Bosnia dozed, and when they got to Bosnia-Herzegovina, she found herself in perfect harmony with the surroundings. The devastation of the villages, buildings, and crops was visible to the naked eye, and she felt as bereft as this abandoned corner of the world. Watching the SFOR trucks skidding in the mud of the ruined roads, she thought, "If I had not found happiness, I would be miserable," because, in her heart along with Mumo, whom she would probably lose, were Adem, Mamouni, Milovan, Hannah, Toscan, Stefan, and Sophie, she counted them on her fingers, and she finally fell sound asleep with their faces scrolling by on the screen of her closed eyelids and turning into little stars that lit up a night so black that she would have been lost without them.

Bosnia wanted to see Mamouni as soon as possible, and Mumo only after. She had woken up with that clear thought, which she shared with Milovan, Adem being asleep. "Of course, my child"—Bosnia loved it when he called her that—"First we'll drop your bags off at my place and have a bite to eat, I have everything we need there." He also had "a few things to take care of" at the jewellery shop and he had to "stash the gold—oh, that Toscan! He's always had a knack for business. I'm going to have to go back to France and see him. You know, I'm more of a homebody myself, I've hardly left the Balkans—in the summer, I go fishing, in the fall, hunting. You know one of the things that upset me the most during the war? It was when I went back to the woods to check my hunting camp, and everything had been destroyed, the cabin, the trees around it, my boat, my jetty on the lake, everything. The motor from my boat was gone, the fishing rods, the rabbit snares, everything. There weren't even any birds left. You see, Bosnia, they always forget that war also destroys the countryside. On television, all you see are images of devastated cities, but war destroys the houses in the country, the trees, the fruit, the flowers and birds. They never talk about that. Do you know what I did when I found that pile of rubble where my 'mansion in the forest,' as I called it, used to be? I rebuilt it!" And Milovan whistled a tune Bosnia didn't know.

She had woken up with a second flash. "Milovan, I've been thinking, before becoming a doctor of the mind, I think I'm going to study philosophy. I want to understand the basis of existence, you know what I mean?" He kept on whistling, while the landscape streamed by in the fog. They weren't very far from Sarajevo now. "As they say, my dear child, you have your whole life ahead of you."

Bosnia had spoken to her mother on the telephone, and when they arrived at her building, she was already at her window on the fifth floor, waving energetically with a cloth, a dishtowel or something, looking like a mythical heroine carved on the prow of a ship to ensure a safe crossing. Without seeing her face, Bosnia knew from this gesture how joyful her Mamouni was. That reminded her of the sad visit she'd made to her only a few months before, but now it seemed like a century, when she had heard only the silence of the cold ward where her mother had sat motionless facing the window, her mother who had been considered crazy and who no longer was. They climbed the stairs four at a time, and when they reached her floor, her mother was in the doorway with her arms wide open like wings to enfold her returning child, the daughter she had missed so much without telling anyone. It was in the evening before going to sleep that she would secretly speak to Sabaheta, or sometimes at night between two dreams, recounting the joys and sorrows of her day in the darkness, and even confiding her worries and fears, because after her daughter's departure, there was a dark place in her heart forged on the anvil of loss, and also because her daughter's departure for a faraway place had made her someone to whom things could be revealed that were hidden from everyone, even from her friend Liliana, and even from herself—as in the old days when she had prayed to God. They held each other without words, without tears, for an eternity of reunion.

Adem and Milovan came quietly into the apartment. Milovan made the introductions, and then Liliana made coffee. And her mother said, "You can't cry all the time! Let's all sit down and have a cup of coffee."

"You can't cry all the time!" Bosnia realized everything that lay behind those words, everything the two of them had gone through and that was between them now that the war was over—her father dead in the forest, the house looted and burned along with the outbuildings, the animals killed—and if they were to name a single one of these losses, the dam would burst and everything would be flooded with tears, they and their friends there with them, the apartment and the building, everything, all Sarajevo and all Bosnia. Now that they had known the fire of war, they did not want to risk a flood.

No, you can't cry all the time. Bosnia moved very close to Adem, she knew his losses too, they had all been in the same tragedy—Liliana, who must have known her share of suffering, and Milovan, and all of them around the delicious coffee and the little cakes. They savoured them, and presented the gifts from France, laughed, and told stories. Until the shadow of Mumo loomed, and they had no choice but to broach the subject.

Basically, it was simple. His mother, Liliana, and Milovan all agreed that Mumo was crazy—and dangerous—and that Bosnia, perhaps with Adem, since they were young like him, should go see him and try to get him to see reason. They all doubted it would work, but after all, they had nothing to lose by trying. Mamouni spoke of her sorrow initially, and then her anger later, oh yes, she resented him for becoming that violent fighter, that embodiment of hate, sometimes she resented him still, some days the sorrow surfaced again, but most of the time, thanks to Liliana, thanks quite simply to the power of life, she was almost indifferent, the war had not defeated her—although reason had run off for a season, and she had never understood how it had gone or how it had returned—the war had left her alive and relatively healthy, and her own son would not defeat her, Insh'Allah! ("It must be hard for a loving mother to reach that point—can you imagine disavowing your own son? No, it's just not possible, it's not in the normal order of things, it's as if a huge desert without oases appeared in the middle of a luxuriant garden, it's just not possible," Bosnia said to Adem later, in their bedroom overlooking the winter garden, at Milovan's. And it occurred to Bosnia that her Mamouni, faced with one hurt too many in the loss of her son Mumo, had become like Mamma Roma in Pasolini's film—which she had seen one afternoon with Hannah—that normal-looking mother who in the desert of her motherhood sat stunned, facing the table on which lay the body of her criminal, crazy son who had died in prison.)

(Hannah had discussed with her the fact that each of the monotheistic religions glorified sacrificed sons: the Jewish religion, Isaac; the Christian religion, none other than God made flesh, Jesus Christ; and the Muslim religion, the martyr, son of Mohammed, reproduced in infinite numbers of suicide bombers.)

That night, Bosnia and Adem hardly slept, they talked and argued, they had an enormous need to analyze things—everything was so complicated, not only things but, especially, people. They saw Mumo the next day and spent a large part of the afternoon with him in his miserable apartment in the filthy suburb, which, in any case, he was preparing to leave—the SFOR soldiers were patrolling everywhere, this country had become hostile, he was leaving with his companions, who were away during Bosnia and Adem's visit, he'd had enough of this "hole," he was going away—where, he didn't say— "Basta, we're going, screw the internationals and the sheep, to hell with them, but when our time comes, we'll be back, yes sir!"

Mumo had become an armoured shell. Bosnia couldn't get over it. How could a human being change so much in such a short time? She tried to cajole him, talked about their childhood, how sweet he had been, his goodness as a little boy, she talked to him about his father and his death among the guerrillas in the Bosnian hills. Adem told him about his time in the barracks with Milovan and their struggle, and his love for Bosnia and their marriage. But it didn't do any good, Mumo was on another planet; with his beard, his long hair, and his bloodshot eyes, he looked like one of those characters in Hollywood science-fiction films, a man fighting a crusade, enraged, unreachable.

And when he spoke, in a steely voice that Bosnia did not recognize, it was only to order his sister to wear the veil, and to declare that when she was fourteen years old, she had dishonoured his family and that they should have stoned her. That was too much! Bosnia said no more. At that precise instant, she made a final break with her brother, sharply, coldly—and she felt that cold, too. As for Adem, feeling the same anger and desire to kill that he had felt toward the bastards who had raped and murdered his family, he said only, "Poor fellow!" He took Bosnia by the hand, and added, "We're leaving." Mumo began to rave, but they could not hear him any more, they were entirely absorbed in themselves, trying in silence to bind the wounds that had been reopened. They did not say a word until they got out to the street, and then they started running as they had when they were kids. Several blocks away, they hugged. Bosnia couldn't get the haunted eyes of her brother out of her mind, but she didn't cry. "You're brave, my love," Adem said as they entered a café. "At least, we're free of him. He's leaving."

That evening, they went to the living room to talk and Milovan joined them—which was actually what they had been hoping for. He offered them coffee and cherry liqueur, which they sipped while smoking cigarettes. They decided then not to hold the planned funeral ceremonies for Adem's family, whose remains they had wanted to repatriate, or for Bosnia's father. They had dreamed of burying them all in the same plot beside Adila and Marina, not far from Bosnia's old building, where the war had created a cemetery that later became a garden, but it was enough, they would come back next summer and take care of Mamouni and those important rituals, they would come back for two months, maybe three, and would be interpreter-guides in the ruins of Sarajevo. Milovan told them some anecdotes about his day, and in the wee hours of the morning before they went to bed, he said, "Well, children, you have a week left. What if we enjoyed ourselves in the time remaining?"

XXX

THE RETURN TRIP was supposed to be quick, but there was a problem with the connecting flight in Frankfurt, so Bosnia and Adem had to spend several hours in the airport, which gave them time to talk without interruption and without pressure, they had so many thoughts and images from the trip and for their plans for the future. They would return to Sarajevo for the whole summer. They already had jobs "interpreting the ruins," as Milovan said, and besides, they wanted to see their city again, and Mamouni and Liliana, and it would be a pleasure to stay with Milovan again—"What a wonderful guy!"—especially since this time he wanted to take them to his "mansion in the forest" to go fishing on the lake in a brand-new boat, to see the trees growing back, to witness the return of the birds. Where would they come from, the new birds? Would there be strange species, specimens never seen before, and would they sing differently? Where do the birds come from after a war? They were eager to see the mountain country again and to stay over there. Then they would ask the SFOR soldiers for help to bring back the remains of their loved ones abandoned in the earth that had run with blood and sweat, tainted ground trampled by the murderers, they would take them back and give them a decent burial beside Adila and Marina, with a ceremony, songs, and readings that they had already thought about.

During their conversation, Bosnia had another tape playing in her head, Mumo's story, which had been with her since their final meeting, but which she hadn't talked to anyone about or even dreamed of any more. She could barely read (these days, she was reading Yourcenar's *The Abyss*, which she had really loved at first, but she could no longer focus on it, she'd get distracted and go back to her own situation). Since seeing Mumo, she kept going over the same scenario again and again, powerless, and abandoning it unresolved, floating in the air without head or tail, hanging threads tangled with all the thoughts she kept to herself. She was elsewhere. Elsewhere, in her head, where she finally articulated what she should have said to Mumo, where she emerged triumphant from a debate in which the truths she spoke dazzled her brother and made him see reason—but she had said nothing, and the tape with the internal monologue started to play again. To a question from Adem, who was concerned about her distracted state—they were sitting at a table at one of the airport snack bars—she finally opened up, without warning, as if that question was all she had been waiting for: "When he was there, Mumo, with his mean eyes, his dirty hair and beard, and when he ordered me to wear the veil, when he accused me of adultery and talked about stoning, I know now what I should have said to him that I didn't."

She saw that Adem was listening closely and continued, "I should have told him right to his face, without being vulgar, but firmly, that the victims of rape aren't the ones who should be punished. The victims of rape, especially when they are children, should be comforted and protected. We need to give them more love, as Mama did when she cradled me, wept with me, and rubbed my whole body with soothing salve. I should have said to him that rapists, of children, of women, and of men, should be punished, and that we would help him and comfort him if he wanted to talk about what the Chetniks had done to his body, that we would take him back into our hearts if he would open up and would stop playing the *mutawaa**   with his sister, who is an autonomous person and doesn't take orders from him, that I have my own ethics and I don't force others to accept my wishes and sexual fantasies, that a people that leaves its rapists unpunished is a people that is digging a huge grave in its own earth, in which its culture will rot. And I should have informed him, in case the news hadn't reached his poor brainwashed mind, that rape in war is already considered a crime under international law, and that one day all rape, in time of war or in time of peace, will be judged a crime against humanity.

---

* An agent empowered by religious authorities to enforce virtue and put down vice in Saudi Arabia.

"And then, if he was not moved by that and if he persisted in his enraged silence, I would have talked about the veil. Isn't it funny, Adem, how the word *veil* in French is *rape* with the vowels reversed: *voile* and *viol*? I would have proven to him logically that his friends' demands regarding women were completely wrong, that if women have to conceal their hair and heads from men's eyes because those parts of the body represent sex, then why do men leave their own sex in plain sight, with their mops of hair and beards displayed for all to see? And I would have said to him that they are basically sex maniacs and perverts, and that it makes me sad but also angry to see the brother I loved so much lost in that sectarian brotherhood."

Bosnia stopped, her cheeks burning. Their flight had been called. Adem hugged her, "I love you, sweetheart, it's good that you talked to me. I would have agreed with you completely. But try not to think about it all the time." And Bosnia, relieved, asked, "Why is it always afterwards that I think of what I should have said when something painful happens to me?" They ran to the gate, they didn't have much time left before it closed. When they were on the plane, comfortable in their seats, they burst out laughing without really knowing why. What they did know, though, was that they loved to travel and they were happy to be going back to France. Their conversation returned to its usual rhythm—sometimes they could spend long periods in silence together, and sometimes the words seemed to pour out of a bottomless well, a well that would never run dry in an entire lifetime. "Dear, I haven't mentioned this to you before, I was waiting for the right time ... I've been thinking about a plan that would involve the two of us, but it's just an idea, I don't know if it will work out, anyway, it's kind of a dream, and for me to pursue it, you would have to be with me in it. At the law faculty, in one of the courses I've been auditing, I've met a fascinating professor, very intelligent and friendly. She's an expert on international law, and the two of us have often talked. She knows the history of the former Yugoslavia and the whole situation in Bosnia-Herzegovina like the back of her hand, it was her territory, she says. I'll introduce her to you one day, her name is Louise H. She's a judge too, and she's willing to take me on in her team, as one of her assistants, but it would mean we would have to leave, because she's returning to her country at the end of the semester. Her country is very far away, it's Canada, and it's really cold there in winter.

"I could study international law at the Université du Québec à Montréal, in the faculty of political science and law—which is excellent, according to Louise H. With what Milovan is offering us for tuition and living expenses, I think we could manage quite well. But Canada is a long way away. It's the province of Quebec, actually, have you heard of it? What do you think of all this?"

Bosnia had absolutely no objections to the plan, and they continued their dialogue. Bosnia had already dreamed of Canada, of the Inuit and the Innu, the Mohawks and the Hurons, the wide-open spaces, the ice floes and the deserts of snow where the only blood you'd see was that of the animals people killed for survival. She had often dreamed of the millions of lakes and the boreal forest, where, when you lived there, you didn't have the time or the desire to think about war, because the landscape forced you to contemplate the end of the world every day. She had often envisioned one day putting an ocean between the old world of wars and the new one that had long been free of murderous atrocities—since the massacres of the aboriginal peoples, that is, of which everyone remained guilty, she supposed. "I know about Canada, yes, but where is Quebec?" Adem laughed. He had only recently learned a little about that country, thanks to Louise H., and, while he was amused by Bosnia's idyllic fantasies, which were shared by millions of people, he was nevertheless delighted that she was open to this plan he had recently been quietly working out. They would have lots of time to learn more about Quebec, and Bosnia, of course, could study philosophy there and train to become a doctor of the mind, they must have philosophers and psychoanalysts in Quebec. In fact, Hannah had mentioned a friend of hers who was a psychoanalyst there, she could introduce her. In the meantime, Louise H. had told him about a very good bookstore in Paris, the Librairie du Québec on Rue Gay-Lussac, not far from the apartment, where they could find more information. Bosnia would discover dozens of writers there.

Adem told her what little he knew about Quebec ... That the French had colonized it in the seventeenth century and that it had been called New France then and included all the lands and waters extending as far as the Mississippi River and Louisiana, until the English-speaking people of the thirteen colonies further south, who had come from Great Britain, conquered the whole area from the Great Lakes to the Gulf of Mexico and made it part of what would become one of the great empires of history. Relations were good between the French colonists and the native peoples (whom the first explorers called Indians because they initially believed they had landed in the Indies), and there was even quite a lot of intermarriage, until the arrival of the armies of the British Empire, who did not succeed in putting down the uprising of the colonies, which gained their independence and formed a republic, the United States, but did impose their law further north, defeating the armies of the king of France and conquering New France. "You know, Bosnia, after the Conquest in 1763, there were sporadic attempts at rebellion by the French of the country, which after Confederation was called Canada and today consists of ten provinces, including Quebec. Just before the Conquest, in 1755, there was a mass deportation of the people called Acadians, but the sons and daughters of the deportees came back. Like the Québécois, they are a people. We'll go and see them in Acadia, it's in the Maritime provinces on the Atlantic coast. In addition to the ten provinces, where the vast majority of people are English-speaking, there are the Inuit territories in the far north, Nunavut and Nunavik."

"Oh, I'd love to go there!" Bosnia said.

"Yes, we'll go, we'll leave for those lands without borders, where the people have been able to live their dream of a country in their language and their religion, and without war for several centuries. Can you imagine it, Bosnia?"

Then they talked about Hannah and Toscan, about the unconditional love they felt for them—like filial devotion and gratitude—but, at the same time, they agreed, they didn't want to impose on them now that Hannah was frail and a housekeeper was going to come and live with them to help her—as Toscan had told them when he had driven them to the airport. The two had decided, when they got back, to speak to them about their decision to move in with Stefan, who had rented a large apartment in the twentieth arrondissement, not as beautiful as Hannah and Toscan's, which was really luxurious, but adequate and, though rather Spartan, well kept by Stefan, who had an artist's eye. It was a bit like growing up and leaving loving parents, and they would manage to find the words to tell Hannah and Toscan without making them feel rejected. "And when you think about it," said Bosnia, "they lived together very happily before us, and even though they adore us, as they say, maybe they'll also be a little bit relieved?" Bosnia and Adem continued talking until they landed, without reading or napping, reliving bits and pieces of what they had experienced in the last week in their wounded Herzegovina.

At the Roissy airport, they were very surprised to see Hannah all smiles beside Toscan. They had imagined her bedridden at home since she had left the hospital, but she walked briskly to meet "my two children," and the members of this family brought together by the vicissitudes of life exchanged joyous hugs and expressions of tenderness. "It's been so long," said Hannah and Toscan. "And what will they say when we talk about America?" the two young people wondered to themselves. (But, some days later, around the table, when they began gently to reveal their dreams and plans for the future, they were met only with tender agreement, and even an astonishing proposal that they go with them soon to the notary in order to be included in their wills. Bosnia and Adem, embarrassed and moved, did not know how to respond. Bosnia finally blurted awkwardly, "What have we done to deserve such generosity? How can we thank you for such kindness? You two, with Milovan, are our heaven on earth." To which Hannah and Toscan, one or the other or both at once, simply replied, "Children, there's no need to look for reasons or to invoke heaven. It's because we love you." And Hannah added, "You know, I dream of seeing Quebec again, and my dear friend Pauline. She's in Rimouski now, and you'll be able to meet her. You'll see, you'll love her. I'll write to her tomorrow, and I'll call her!") The four of them headed towards the parking lot, talking all the while.

Hannah seemed much better. She had resumed her favourite activities: playing the piano, cooking, reading, going to films and museums, and seeing her few friends. A housekeeper had been hired, a woman about fifty years old from Romania, a widow with two grown children who had stayed back home, she wanted to be called Nana, she was pretty, very witty and cultivated, and spoke four languages in addition to Romanian— German, English, Russian, and French (her favourite). They had put her in a small room that had formerly been Toscan's office, and when the children left, she would have their rooms in the garret. "But you'll always have a home here when you come back to Paris, the little bedroom will be for you," Hannah said, like a mother whose children had returned home— she loved that idea. One evening, they organized a celebration for Pesach,* and Sophie and Stefan were invited. Nana did the shopping and cooked Hannah's recipes. Toscan, as always, took care of the wine, and at the table, he was the one who carved the leg of lamb. After the meal, Hannah sat down at the piano to accompany Nana, who had a beautiful voice and knew all the folk songs of central Europe.

For the Easter holiday, the four of them, Hannah, Toscan, Bosnia, and Adem, drove south, visited the Rhône valley, then went through Avignon and Cavaillon, and crossed the Lubéron at Manosque, where they stayed for a week. One day, on Mont d'Or, which Bosnia and Adem had climbed on foot to picnic and dream—one day with no mistral, so they could contemplate in peace, hear themselves think, even make out the beating of the wings of butterflies coming back to life among the scrubby vegetation—as they stood shoulder to shoulder, silent, dazzled, with so many

—

* The Jewish holiday of Passover.

recollections of so many things that had happened since the first time they made that climb two seasons ago, Adem suddenly said, "We've come a long way and it's been a very long time," and Bosnia agreed. Projecting herself into the uncertain future that awaited them, she took from her backpack one of the books she had bought at the Librairie du Québec and read, "I'll die without dying. Lark, quail, canary, when you return from the sun, when you come flying back to your dying homeland, your shadows etched against the uneven terrain, sing, I beg of you, sing yourselves hoarse." Those were the last lines in Jacques Brault's beautiful book *Death-Watch.**

Bosnia asked Adem, "Are you beginning to understand where we're going?"

---

* Translated by David Lobdell.

Part Three

QUEBEC

XXXI

THERE WAS A HUGE WINDOW, through which Bosnia was gazing into the distance, into an infinite whiteness, all that snow, that absolute silence interspersed with muffled sounds. She thought, "This is how I imagine eternity, the music of eternity, not darkness or monotony, but the dazzling white of the sun and the patterns of shadows under smoke from chimneys, shadows that write unknown words, that scribe notes unheard by mortals, which we will be able to read on the other slope of life, when our breath has left these poor bodies that are unable to fly." The crackling of the fire in the hearth brought her back to the warm room where Pauline sat reading in an old armchair, a woollen blanket over her legs, the lamp lighting the book and her hands, with their skin like parchment, and setting her grey hair aglow so that it looked like the tufts of sweet clover that grow wild in July. Most of all, it brought Bosnia back to the warm body of Adem beside her, who was completely absorbed in the dancing flames while he stroked Bosnia's hair and she, her ear pressed against his body, listened to his breathing and the beating of his heart. He was her Adem, her love, and they had come such a long way, the two of them. "A lifetime would not be enough to tell of everything we have experienced since we left France, the heart-rending goodbyes to Hannah and Toscan—but they will come and see us as soon as we're settled, they'll come and see us, they promised—and the return to Sarajevo, where we spent the summer as 'guides of the ruins,' and where we wept with Mamouni and Milovan and Liliana in our makeshift cemetery, and also where we celebrated and sang and went back to Milovan's 'mansion in the forest,' which we named 'the mansion that is no more,' and the birds were the same and they sang as they did in the past—where did they go during the war?" Bosnia reflected, and her gaze went back to the window, where she could see the St. Lawrence River and the long black line in the middle marking a lost continent, St. Barnabé Island, whose name she had seen on a map, and then beyond it, endless whiteness to the line of the horizon, very far in the northwest, a glimpse of the country on the other side, the North Shore, but "it's still the same country, it's still Quebec," they had told her with pride.

It seemed to her then that the immensity of this land and water was on a scale with the irrational hope she felt about life, immense enough for one to bury any sorrows one might wish to forget under the drift ice—which melts in the spring, of course, it was not possible to magically wipe past horrors from memory or to anaesthetize the part of the soul where atrocities have found a hiding place. But the other day, walking on the ice with Adem, both of them deep in the untranslatable silence of the horrors they had experienced in Bosnia-Herzegovina, she had felt that, here, she was finally burying her father and her dear Adila and Marina under the ice. Bosnia had whispered this to Adem, who, in this landscape at the very limits of the imaginable, had not seemed the least bit surprised, he had just taken Bosnia's mitten in his own and squeezed her hand, and Bosnia had seen in the icy air the smoky arabesque of his breath, writing his eternal assent.

While Adem went to put wood on the fire in the fireplace, Bosnia was transported back to the time of the daily struggle to find fuel, the time before Adem, when she and Adila and Marina would huddle together near the fire of the books from their dwindling library and tell each other as many stories as there were hours to survive. Here in this cozy living room in Rimouski, where Hannah's psychoanalyst friend had retired after a life of "joys and labours" in Montreal and Paris, here in this peaceful Nordic silence of late afternoon where night falls in the middle of the day, at about 4 P.M., so that you are pushed unprepared into the time of the next day, where it seems natural with every sunset to leap into eternity without dying, Bosnia turned from the window, the tableau outside having been erased by the sudden darkness, and heard the crackling of the fire and the rustling of the pages of the book Pauline was reading and was carried back to the pages consumed in the makeshift hearth in the little apartment in Sarajevo. She thought of the book Hannah had given her, which she had just finished reading, *Liquidation*, by the Hungarian

Jew Imrc Kcrtész, who had been in Auschwitz, where many of his compatriots were murdered, and who had said, "Even if I am seemingly speaking about something completely different, I am speaking about Auschwitz." And Bosnia felt that, in spite of all the ice floes of the world under which she would like to bury the horror, she would always carry within her her wounded Herzegovina. Touching her belly, in which she once again recognized the little cyclical pains, she said to herself yet again, "Ah, not pregnant, what a relief, I must tell Adem right away, I'm not ready to carry a child, Adem and I aren't ready, too much healing to do, and too much building!" She headed to the kitchen to join Pauline, who had put aside her book, whose title Bosnia had glimpsed in passing: *Enchantment and Sorrow: The Autobiography of Gabrielle Roy*. Pauline had told her, during their walk on the boardwalk by the river that looked like the bridge of a steamship, that she only liked "books written in poetry," whether they were novels, biographies, essays, or poems. Bosnia would help Pauline with supper and Adem would uncork the wine, a Pommard from Toscan that they had brought with them. On the menu was a leg of lamb—Pauline had decided to celebrate with "all my children," and they would soon go to the bus station to pick up her daughter Valérie, who was studying history at Laval University and was coming to spend her February reading week in Rimouski.

"I have three mothers," thought Bosnia, "Mamouni, Hannah, and now Pauline." She kissed Pauline on the cheek and Adem on the neck. The aroma of the lamb roasting in the oven reminded her of the big Hajj celebration at her maternal grandparents' house after Ramadan. But she did not cry, she simply felt what she had long believed was reserved for other people— happiness—as if her tears had frozen under the ice with everything else buried there, until spring and, perhaps, she hoped, until the end of everything, when nothing in the body moved any longer, or suffered.

XXXII

WHEN THEY HAD ARRIVED in Montreal in September, after returning from Sarajevo and spending a short time with Hannah and Toscan in Paris, Bosnia and Adem had at first been taken in by a Croat family who were friends of Stefan's family. Then, quite quickly, after crisscrossing the city and knocking on the doors of all the centres for immigrants and refugees from throughout the world, they had found a perfect little apartment in the Plateau Mont-Royal neighbourhood, an area teeming with vitality and youth. They shared the apartment with a roommate as was a common practice in Quebec, a charming young man named Cédric who was from the Gaspé and was studying theatre. Together they had unrolled a map and looked at how big this country was, and then placed a map of their little Bosnia-Herzegovina beside it. "You had a war just for that little area?" asked Cédric. "Really, I don't understand." And he put his finger on a point in the upper Gaspé Peninsula. "You see, that's where I come from, there right on the sea—it's the Gulf of St. Lawrence, but we call it the sea—nearly opposite Anticosti Island, which is shaped like a fish. It's full of moose and deer, and there are lots of trout and salmon in the rivers. You'll have to come next summer. And one day we'll go to Europe together, but maybe not to Bosnia, I'm afraid of war." Cédric read them poems by Anne Hébert and stories by Jacques Ferron, a great writer and also a doctor, who had lived in his village. Adem had enrolled in political science and law at UQAM, he had liked the professors he had met and got on well with the students he encountered.

Soon he would take the bus back to Montreal. He had come to Rimouski with Bosnia, who had decided to give herself a year of freedom, without studies and without any plans other than to let the seasons express their own designs. Bosnia was filled with hope. "I don't know why," she told Adem, "but what I see seems immeasurably more hopeful to me than all the disasters that have been accumulating in my heart for so long." She was silent for a moment, then added very softly, "I don't have the words to express all my thoughts, all the shapes, the depths and the heights. One day, Adem, I will find those words, they will articulate the tragedies, but also the delights, the wonders. Or if I paint, I will find the colours." Then she read Adem the words of the American poet Stanley Kunitz at the funeral service for the painter Mark Rothko, in New York on February 28, 1970: "Not all the world's corruption washes his colors away." And Adem, taking Bosnia in his arms, felt his love for her as vast as this country where they had ended up, and gave her all the space she wanted to fulfill the extraordinary promises of time.

One evening in Montreal, when they were drinking jasmine tea and listening to fado—Cédric and his friend

Jean-Philippe had chosen the music—and looking through the huge curtainless window at the sky of the city, the lighting in the buildings, and the traffic lights drawing stars and constellations as if with red chalk, Bosnia rediscovered the ghosts of her nostalgia. Resurrected by the fado, they horrified and yet mesmerized her, and she saw again, as if it were happening in the present, the exhumation of her father in that forest where she had fought at his side and where she had buried him and covered him with her invisible veil to the sound of a Bach partita in her inner ear, and recited the Al-Lat lament: "In the Name of God, the All-Mothering, the Merciful." That time seemed so far away, farther than America from Bosnia-Herzegovina, and yet it was there in that instant of the nostalgic fado—she was holding Adem's hand and looking at the two young Canadian SFOR soldiers who had accompanied them just in case, she heard the birds singing and the young soldier Julien asking in a voice filled with choked-back tears, "How can the birds sing here? It seems impossible, almost blasphemous." Later, on the road back to Sarajevo, Bosnia held to her belly the tin box Milovan had made, which contained her father's remains, caressing it, warming it with her warm hands in the July sun as if it were alive, an infant just delivered from the womb of the earth, and she did not cry, did not speak, only hummed her Al-Lat lament from a time that was past yet still present. The young soldier Julien had said he had heard this in a course he had taken in Kingston, Ontario, entitled "Memories of War," with a professor who was a writer, and that it was what the war correspondent Matthew Halton of the CBC had said when he had first reported on the horrors of the Nazi death camp in Meppen, Germany, in April 1945.

"How can the birds sing here?" Bosnia heard simultaneously with the Bach partita and the nostalgic fado, and she saw again the scene of her father's second burial in that makeshift graveyard where two years before they had laid the bodies of Adila and Marina, hand in hand. There was her Mamouni, who was crying, and Milovan and Liliana and Adem standing on the ruined stones and dry grass. The hot sun defied sorrow, the leaves had grown back on the trees so recently charred by weapon fire, a yellow primrose still grew against the wall that shimmered in the sweltering heat, and there were the birds, still and always. Adem seemed so absent that afternoon, elsewhere, unreachable—the SFOR soldiers had forbidden them to go to the sector where Adem had buried his mother, his father, his grandmother, his uncle, and his little sisters Aida and Malenka; the area, now the property of the Bosnian Serb Republic, had been mined, the soil covering death reseeded with death. Adem could no longer even think about the macabre discovery he had once made, nor about his family or the dog Milo, which he had also buried, and when he came back from his macabre thoughts, he said to Bosnia and Milovan, "If I think about it, I'll go mad." And who, wondered Bosnia, could ever cure such madness?

So on that evening of fado, she had devised a plan, a plan to go to the ocean—she wanted to go to the end of the world of America, across from Europe, to go there with Adem from Rimouski, where they would rent a car. After all, hadn't Cédric told them when they were looking at the map of the Gaspé Peninsula that at the end was Gaspé, and that Gaspé, in the Mi'kmaq language of its original inhabitants, was Gespeg, meaning "the end of the earth"? In Gaspé, at the end of the pier for sea-going ships, she would look toward Europe just across the water, and at the wall of the open sea, she would cry out, she would scream at that old land of wars sown with ancient blood, she would bawl her unfathomable sorrow, she would howl her mourning, but no one would hear her over the roar of the high waves, no one but Adem, who, silent, would feel a dull echo rising from the crater dug deep within him.

XXXIII

BOSNIA DID NOT KNOW WHY, but she felt like telling Valérie about her last meeting with Mumo in the ruins of Sarajevo. The two of them were sitting on the highest peak in the Matapédia region, near Val-d'Irène, contemplating the astonishing wild beauty of the valley far below, the rounded outlines of the lake and the hills and valleys as far as St-Tharcicius and St-Vianney, and even farther, following the line of the Matane River past Mont Blanc in the Appalachians, all the way to the gulf. Perhaps because the panorama reminded Bosnia of the Dinaric Alps of her childhood before the war, perhaps also because Valérie had talked to her about her own childhood, which had been as tranquil as this setting so distant from the troubles and horrors Bosnia had witnessed, a childhood consisting only of the everyday joys of life—was it possible?—with the occasional excitement like butterfly wings leaving fleeting dark shadows, and because Valérie, pointing to the village of Amqui below, had said, as if in a happy dream, "You see the church, there, look just to the left of the steeple and then turn towards the river and go a quarter of a kilometre, and there, that beautiful house among the trees, right by the water, do you see it? That was the home of my grandparents, Maman's parents, they were wonderful, I loved them." Bosnia had heard "I loved them" as if it were part of a faraway story from the *Thousand and One Nights*, and she had wondered, "Where does it come from, when one has been pampered and happy, this need Valérie has to travel the world, to study the history and stories of humanity, to grasp the destiny of human beings from every angle, the good and the bad. Where does she get this passion to understand the greed and viciousness as well as the goodness and kindness? Valérie has a mother who's very close to her, who pays for everything she needs to go to school, lends her her car so we can drive around as much as we like this week, who is erudite and understanding, who practised her profession as a psychoanalyst with passion, who was and still is beautiful, who married 'for form, that's how it was done here back then,' who separated and divorced when she didn't love her man any more, who had other casual lovers and 'a few loves,' as she said softly. Where does this freedom come from, like a gift from life?" Cradled in the beauty of the surroundings, facing the dizzying enigma of the lives of Valérie and her mother Pauline, she felt a kind of lightness, a feeling that was the complete opposite of the nostalgic fado, something close to the pure trust she had felt in childhood before the rape when she was fourteen and before the war, and although she knew deep inside that there must be turbulence and suffering beneath the idyllic image of her new country, she savoured the blessings of the moment, and she began to tell the final chapter of Mumo's story, which until then only Mamouni, Milovan, Liliana, Adem, Hannah, and Toscan knew.

XXXIV

WHEN SHE ENTERED the makeshift shelter within the ruins, surrounded by other ruins, Bosnia did not immediately recognize the human shape leaning motionless against the only stone wall still standing, dressed in a strange outfit like the rags of a medieval peasant, a relic snatched from some open grave, the eyes dull and empty, the hair shaggy, already white, the beard yellowed. She did not realize at first glance that this was her brother Mumo, four years her elder, who already looked like the old men you'd sometimes see wandering around Brusa Bezistan Bazaar or the old Gazi Husrev Bey Mosque, if they were still able to walk—if not, they were put in the insane asylum, like those she had seen on her visits to Mamouni when she was sick from too much death everywhere. She did not understand that this human thing with its vacant stare was her brother Mumo. And then, suddenly, she knew and was dumbfounded by that knowledge, she knew in an instant when she slowly approached him, holding on to Adem with a trembling hand, and searched those blank eyes for the least little spark of the old light, she realized—as something deep inside her had known as soon as they entered the shelter—that this was her brother Mumo, she knew it when he looked at her and she saw a fleeting glimmer of light, and when the single word "library" came from the mouth hidden behind the beard, she knew because she recognized that glimmer, and because his voice had not changed.

She cried "Mumo," and her voice reverberated among the crumbling stones, she repeated "Mumo," but her brother had returned to his darkness, and her thoughts began to race in her head and crash down upon her heart like stones. She did not want this ordeal, and wished she hadn't come here with Adem, but it was too late, she was here. "Tell me I'm dreaming," she said, but Adem did not answer, could not answer, he too had been plunged into nightmares of the war and regretted having come. But he had given in to the pleas of Mamouni to bring her "big boy" back, obsessed as she was since the call had come from the ambassador in Bucharest informing them of Mumo's return to Bosnia-Herzegovina. Apparently, he had crossed Moldavia on foot. Some unknown person had got him out of Dagestan, where he had been imprisoned and tortured after the training camp where he had gone to learn to fight and kill infidels was destroyed and his comrades murdered. Mamouni, accompanied by Milovan, had seen her son once and had not recognized him—the only words he had spoken to her were "alone here" and "library," and she had not understood what he meant. Mumo had violently pushed Mamouni and Milovan out of the shelter, as he was doing now to Bosnia and Adem, fighting them like an animal attacked in its lair, shouting with such fury that they decided never to try to see him again. Occasionally, someone they knew would spot him begging on the banks of the Miljacka and would throw him some fruit, bread, or scraps of meat or fish—he usually came out after the muezzin's call, "Allah Akbar," and would stow the alms in a ragged old bag and return blindly to his shelter.

"You see, Valérie, I knew that day that I wanted never again to live in Bosnia-Herzegovina, as if a great love that had existed had come to an end, and I knew that I would never understand our last meeting or why Mumo, who had never had any interest in books, who had never wanted to study, had kept in his mouth only that single word "library." Was it the memory of the pages we had seen go up in flames that terrible night when our enemies burned the Sarajevo National Library, the oldest and most beautiful library in the Balkans? Was it the memory of the next day, when we all walked dazed through the ashes finding bits of blackened paper printed centuries ago with a few letters still legible on them, the remains of that treasure many people had known nothing of and had discovered only when it was destroyed?" Then a thought crossed Bosnia's mind: it was the day after that insanity that Mumo had had his first attack of "mystical madness," as Milovan called it. Bosnia had never made the connection, but she did not understand what it could mean, nor did she understand the enigma of Mumo's madness, or of any madness. She knew she would carry that mystery with her to the end of her days.

XXXV

THAT MORNING, the port of Montreal was bathed in the pink light of dawn over the black and white snow on the riverbanks. Bosnia let her gaze wander from the Jacques Cartier Bridge on the east to the Champlain Bridge on the west, and beyond, to Mount St. Hilaire, Mount St. Bruno, and Mount St. Grégoire, which she could make out clearly, as far as the hazy outlines of the mountains of the Eastern Townships and even some in the United States, far away in New Hampshire and Vermont. She had sat down on a low concrete wall near containers of all colours, huge trucks loading and unloading, and ocean liners and freighters returning from or leaving for faraway lands. She had always loved railway stations and airports, those places teeming with human activity, and since the tragic year when she was fourteen, and especially during the war, imagining herself elsewhere had always been a means of survival for her. After her stay in France and her sad return to Sarajevo, she had wanted more than anything else to go to a country she would never leave. They had come to Quebec, she and Adem, and they had loved what they had found here right from the start. For the first time in a long time, she wanted to put down roots, to find an address, a home, and—leaving aside travelling, which she would always treasure as much as books—she felt a need never to go away again. Which did not prevent her from cultivating that part of herself that had made her what she was now, from faithfully paying tribute to the memory of the desire to leave that was so much a part of her, the invisible fibres in the organs of her body, the muscles, nerves, and tendons that could not be seen but were just as vital as breath, tears, blood, or sweat. That was why, in this city that was chosen and not imposed by birth or deportation, why, even while staying here, she travelled every day, on foot or by bus or subway, from east to west and north to south. She had begun with the main arteries, St. Laurent and Sherbrooke—people had told her, "You'll see, Montreal is built like a cross"—wandering with her backpack, unfolding her map on a café table, on a park bench, or on her knees, as was the case today as she sat watching all the arrivals and departures. Through the sounds of motors and clanking metal and men shouting, she thought she could make out the music of the cracking ice—unlike in the Lower St. Lawrence region, it wasn't called drift ice here—it was March, the promise of spring could be heard even in the symphony of the ice, and she wrote in her notebook, "The lament of the ice because winter is leaving." She always had a book in her bag, she was learning about Quebec through the books of past and present, and along with the map, she always carried her pocket dictionary and the notebook in which she wrote drafts of her letters to Mamouni and to Hannah and Toscan, and cards to Sophie and Stefan and to Valérie and Pauline, with whom she was forming friendships. She did not know clearly yet what she was going to "do with her life," as Mamouni had asked her in her last letter. She had answered, "Dear Mamouni, dear Mama of my heart"— in Bosnian, those words were so tender, as if they carried her right back into Mamouni's arms, a little girl—"My life is now." And she had added, "My life is now and I would like you to come share it, with Adem and me. You'll see, it will be good for you. We'll introduce you to some Bosnians who have come here as refugees, there are several thousand in Montreal and about twelve hundred in Quebec City. Quebec City is supposed to be very beautiful, like a museum high up overlooking the great river. We're going there soon. You know, Adem and I can make the arrangements, it's complicated, but we can manage. How can you still live among all those ruins and all those bad memories, close to your child who has gone mad, how can you?" Bosnia had mailed the letter the day before at the Plateau post office on Papineau, and she was waiting for Mamouni's answer, but she already knew it, it was always the same: "My dear Little Sabaheta, I can't leave your father all alone in his Sarajevo earth, I can't leave my Ismet without my footsteps on the earth where he rests or my hands and my tears regularly warming him. Do you understand, my dear daughter? Since the death of our Ismet, Allah has asked only one thing of me, and that is that I remain among the 'ruins,' as you say, that I live here with the survivors and sow my ever-present memory in your papa's ashes." Mamouni continued, giving news of everyone and describing her days and evenings and her nights punctuated with dreams—with time, the nightmares were gradually subsiding. She ended with love and kisses, and as always, one last question: "My dear child, what are you going to do with your life?"

Bosnia smiled, knowing that her life was now, in the day that was dawning, the films and plays she had seen with Cédric since her arrival, and her love for Adem, whom she cherished more and more, Adem, still taken up with his studies, the fascinating but difficult courses he told her about sometimes. On the weekends, they had little parties with Cédric's friends or Adem's classmates. Bosnia was discovering the culinary arts. She had bought some cookbooks—some classics, including one by Jehane Benoît, and a new one everybody was talking about—and she was practising. Cédric's specialty was desserts. He talked about the current celebrity chef the way someone might hold forth on Homer or Shakespeare or Orson Welles. Adem chose the wines, proud to show off what he had learned from Toscan, and sometimes, when joy caught him unawares, he would cook them up a goulash that they were sure was the "best goulash in all the Balkans," and the only dish he knew how to make—he'd got the recipe from his mother, who had learned it from her grandmother. How could she tell Mamouni that ever since she had left the blood-soaked earth of Europe with Adem, this was her life, and her future would always be now? But in her letters, Bosnia continued to tell her about the process they were going through to acquire refugee status and Canadian citizenship. And she explained to her how these two countries in one, Canada and Quebec, which she had trouble understanding, were constantly negotiating and squabbling, but never with weapons— "It's unimaginable, Mamouni, they attack each other with words that you would find terrible, but they don't kill each other, they don't even imprison each other, they fight with the texts of laws. I'm trying to understand. Adem is learning a lot at university, and he explains to me as best he can." She also told Mamouni about her plans to go back to school in September. Since she already knew Serbo-Croatian, her own language, which was now called Bosnian in Herzegovina, and German and Italian, and of course French—more and more, because of France and Quebec and their literature—she was thinking of going to McGill University to study English language and literature and translation. She could perhaps earn her living as an interpreter or translator or a language teacher. She and Adem had decided to keep the inheritance from Hannah and Toscan to pay for tuition and books, travel, and a little car, which they would buy in the spring, because they wanted to experience this vast country. They also planned to return to Bosnia-Herzegovina and France every year—and to go everywhere in the world, to explore it country by country, the skies, the rivers, and the oceans.

Bosnia told all this to Mamouni, but she knew deep down that for Mamouni—and this kept coming back like a leitmotif—"doing something with your life" meant having children with a man who worked to provide for you. So, as she was doing today after coming back up from the port to sit in a café on Park Avenue, a neighbourhood she was fond of because of its mix of ethnic groups and languages, where she felt at home because it was like being elsewhere, she would write to Hannah and tell her everything she couldn't tell Mamouni. She told Adem too, of course, but words to a lover are different from letters to a distant friend, so she could read him her letters, because with Hannah she would sketch out thoughts she had not yet formulated even to herself, and the written words helped her understand them, she realized as she wrote. She talked about her sometime intention to study philosophy and about the reading she had done before the war, at the University of Sarajevo, which had awakened her interest in it—works by Plato and Kant— and more recently, those of Nietzsche, which she had discovered in Pauline's library in Rimouski. She also spoke of her desire in recent years to understand the universe of madness—after all, her own mother had been mad throughout the war, and her brother Mumo seemed to have gone permanently mad, and Adem, even Adem, after finding his family's heads impaled on stakes, their bodies thrown in the river, and his dog gutted, had for weeks and months experienced darkness in daylight and had nightmares every night. "And what about me," continued Bosnia to Hannah, "am I immune? Shouldn't I immerse myself in that incomprehensible universe, starting from Socrates' first precept, to know yourself?" Hannah answered Bosnia's letters with long letters of her own, letters that "rendered the enigma to the enigma" and that Bosnia kept as treasures.

XXXVI

BOSNIA, ADEM, PAULINE, AND VALÉRIE were sitting in silence on the bank of the Squatec River where it widens into a lake, on a natural beach across from an island where several canoes were moored. In the silence of the forest and the water, from time to time, one of them would say a word, a phrase, no more, punctuated by the lapping of the water or the wings of a partridge deep in the woods. They had come here to the highlands of Témiscouata by mutual agreement, without much discussion, they had decided to leave the St. Lawrence to come greet the spring here and admire the migrating birds, the snow geese and Canada geese that, now in May, were celebrating the sky and the light. First they heard their calls in the south, then they could see flocks of them in full flight northward or getting ready to land to refuel, their movements perfected over the centuries, memorized, like the routes they followed, passed on from generation to generation—and the group on the shore of the lake wondered how, and they interspersed their fascinated contemplation with attempts to explain the phenomenon, without knowing anything about ornithology but simply having succumbed to the sublime magic and the music of the spectacle.

The week before, at the end of Adem's term at university—which had gone very well—Cédric and his friend Jean-Philippe had bought a little car, a shiny red Echo, and left for the Gaspé. And Bosnia and Adem had received another invitation from Pauline, who was expecting Valérie for the entire month of May. Drawn by a desire for salt water, wide-open spaces, and clean air, Bosnia and Adem had also got into a holiday mood, and had headed down along the St. Lawrence. On their first glimpse of the river and Île d'Orléans, it was clear to them why the Mi'kmaq used to call the St. Lawrence "the road that keeps walking all by itself to the sea," as they had read in a book written in the seventeenth century.* They had thought the time on the road would give them a chance to finalize their plans for the summer, but it had taken the entire drive on the dismal highway between Montreal and Quebec City—why, Pauline asked later, hadn't they taken the 132, which runs parallel to it and is so beautiful, but they hadn't known—it had taken those two and a half long hours to dispel the pain they had been feeling since reading the letter they had received from Stefan and Sophie two days earlier. The letter reproached them for their "life that has become too easy," with all the money they'd received from Hannah and Toscan and, even before that, from Milovan, and for having "fled their

—

* Chrestien Leclercq, *Nouvelle relation de la Gaspesie* (translation).

responsibility to their people and turned their backs on France, the land of human rights and liberty." As they travelled, their sadness had turned to anger. It felt as if it would take them years to understand this human propensity to envy the happiness or success of others, and this need to keep suffering when one has once felt pain, as if the remedy for the ordeals of the past was to endlessly atone for them. Soon, however, the magnificence of the landscape transformed their anger into compassion. "They must still be in a lot of pain to criticize us this way," they said, knowing that the four of them would have to have a frank talk when they went to Paris in August, after Bosnia spent a month in Sarajevo while Adem did an internship his thesis director had arranged for him at the International Tribunal for the Prosecution of War Crimes Committed in Former Yugoslavia in The Hague. Yes, they'd have to have a serious discussion with their friends, even if it meant giving up their friendship.

Their mood was serene again when they arrived at Pauline's house. The joy of their reunion was tangible, visible, audible, as they threw themselves into each other's arms and gave each other kisses mingled with laughter. They exchanged greetings and news while unloading their baggage and removing coats and scarves, all of them talking at once but managing to make themselves heard. A bottle of wine was uncorked and glasses brought out for a toast, it was going to be a party, it was one already, and the air was filled with joking and laughter. Pauline said she was in a "country mood" that evening, "It's my fado, my music for celebration and nostalgia," and Bosnia realized that country and western and fado were on the same wavelength, touching the same nerves, striking the same inner chords, even though not many people saw the connection, they simply didn't hear it. Valéric was at the stove, she had made her fish casserole, with snow crab, which had just come in, they would be celebrating its arrival, and in three weeks they would be celebrating the lobster season—so many celebrations, thought Bosnia and Adem. Pauline put on some homegrown Quebec country and western music, and was talkative all evening, as they all were. Adem had a quieter temperament but he also had a good sense of humour, and that evening, he was droll, even hilarious, during the meal and through the numerous bottles of wine they drank while building castles in the air. Pauline told them she was planning to spend two months in France with Hannah and Toscan if Hannah's health did not permit her to take the long trip here that she always enjoyed. She missed her dear friend: "You realize, kids, that we've been needing each other for almost forty years now, it's incredible, isn't it, forty years of unbroken friendship, can you imagine?" And she told them how lucid the friendship was, how filled with true affection, and how Toscan had never interfered in it, and how, over the years, their esteem for each other had been the cement of their relationship. And how neither Hannah nor Toscan had been afflicted by that disease of old age that struck so many of their generation, that dread when confronted with aging, that path of fear and denial that led to snares and deceptions, and how that disease of old age concealed a terrible fear of death. Still to the sound of the country music filled with longing— she had an incredible music collection that covered many periods, countries, cultures, and genres—Pauline read to them from an article she had cut out of a newspaper, which she took from an accordion file filled with clippings: "Hope is a feeling that is sufficient unto itself. To hope, as one eats and drinks, in order to live, to go on living in spite of everything and in spite of death that lurks everywhere. To allow oneself an act of faith without a god, only human, to have hope in hope, in the hope that there is still hope, here, elsewhere, somewhere."*

That evening, which they extended into the wee hours of the morning, putting on the different kinds of music each of them felt like hearing, they agreed on a plan for a little trip to the highlands of Témiscouata. They would leave in two days and drive to Cabano, and they would spend tomorrow taking it easy, doing some shopping, going for a walk, and in the evening, preparing a picnic, "which will be no small thing," promised Pauline, "you'll see." They would take everything they needed for the whole day, and come back late in the evening by the road along the river near Trois-Pistoles, by way of St-Jean-de-Dieu. However, two days later, when they stopped for lunch in Squatec, it was so beautiful and the weather so nice that they decided to go no further, and to see Cabano another

—

* Éric Fottorino, "Oser l'espérance" ["Dare to Hope"], *Le Monde*, January 6, 2004 (translation).

time. They knew, as soon as they got to the church square and stopped in the grove of trees between the church and presbytery and the Squatec River that there was so much here to discover that they would spend their whole trip here. Then they found a place to picnic and watch the migrating birds, on the little natural beach on the river that was like a lake, across from an island. When Valérie asked a passerby, an old man from the village, he had told them that *Escoateg* was a Mi'kmaq or Maliseet word meaning "the source of a river," and he named all the lakes around there, there were so many, and they knew right away, even before they laid out their picnic, hearing the hundreds of birds of different species that they distinguished only by ear in the deciduous and coniferous trees, and the sound of the river rushing below. And Bosnia, enthralled by what she saw here—the sky, the woods, the river, the church and presbytery on a large lot set back from the road, asked, "What are all these birds? I've never heard so many species of birds and so many birdsongs outside the forest on the seven hills surrounding Sarajevo. Where do they come from? And how is it that they're the same ones you hear in Bosnia Herzegovina?" No one answered, they were all savouring the beauty of the place. And Bosnia knew then and there, like the revelation she'd had while with the guerrillas, when her beloved father died, she knew in a single sentence, as true as life or death—and she would tell it to Adem later when they were alone, and she would write it to Hannah soon, but also, she would whisper it in Mamouni's ear when she took her in her arms in

Sarajevo, in the big bedroom in the apartment where she was living with Liliana, when she hugged her as she had done when she was small, and Mamouni would smile with that air of trepidation at life wide open all around her—a sentence that was a self-evident truth for Bosnia, and she repeated it very softly, only to herself: "I know what I'm going to do with my life—I'm going to write, and the first thing I'm going to write is a novel called *The Birds of Squatec.*"

Paris, October 2003 – Rimouski, February 2005